Dash Black. The sexiest man on earth.

Tess moved beneath the silky sheets, her body pleasantly warm from their amazing lovemaking earlier. Dash lay beside her breathing gently. She wanted to get up, call all her friends with the news. Why not? It was her bed, after all. He was a guest. A lover.

Her lover. If she wanted him to be.

Could she just have a fling? Or would she end up losing? She was half in love with him already. Then what? Long lonely nights wishing he was with her? Jealousy every time she saw him in the *National Enquirer?*

It was foolish to get involved with him. What could he possibly see in Tess from tiny Tulip, Texas, who was trying to make it in the Big Apple?

Dash wasn't going to fall in love with her. This was about fun and sex. Sex and more sex. Which was by no means a bad thing. As long as she didn't confuse it with love. If she said yes to the sex part, what did all the rest matter? He belonged in her bed...*and boy, did Dash belong in her.*

"So to do Dash," she whispered. "Or not to do Dash?" She grinned and gazed over at his nude body.

Even in the dark he was a beautiful man. With that sculpted chin, strong nose and eyes that made grown women weep.

All in her bed. Hers. Tess from Tulip, Texas.

Blaze™

To: My Favorite Reader
From: Jo Leigh
Re: *A Dash of Temptation*

So, now that I've got your attention, I want to first thank you for buying the book. My family (me, gorgeous hunk of a boyfriend, three kitties) is thrilled to pieces. Second, I want to tell you about some fun you can have with this cool series. We've not only written the first three books (Alison Kent's *The Sweetest Taboo,* my *Dash of Temptation* and Isabel Sharpe's *A Taste of Fantasy),* we've also made an interactive Web site! Go to http://www.MenToDo.com. Then join in! Tell us about your experience with a Man To Do Before You Said I Do. Share about a Man You'd Like To Do. Vote on the Man We'd All Like To Do. Chat with other folks who've read the books. Check out the fabulous links. Talk about books you'd like to see in the series. This is fun…this is wild… this is BLAZE!

I'll see you online!

Best,

Jo Leigh

A DASH OF TEMPTATION

Jo Leigh

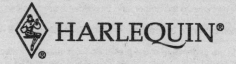

TORONTO • NEW YORK • LONDON
AMSTERDAM • PARIS • SYDNEY • HAMBURG
STOCKHOLM • ATHENS • TOKYO • MILAN • MADRID
PRAGUE • WARSAW • BUDAPEST • AUCKLAND

To Lawrence, who is my Man To Keep

ISBN 0-373-79076-7

A DASH OF TEMPTATION

Copyright © 2003 by Jolie Kramer.

Prologue

To: Erin
CC: Samantha
From: TessThePlantLady@hotmail.com
Subject: Men I'm NOT Going To Do!

Okay, picture this: I'm with Brad. He's wearing Armani and he smells like cashmere on ice. His hair is perfect, including the obligatory rakish bangs across his forehead. His frown is fetching, his gaze hurt.

Me: I'm sorry, Brad. I just can't do this. I want more from a relationship than you can give.
Him: Oh, Tess. You've made me realize you're the only woman in the world for me. I'd be lost without you. (He drops to one knee and whips out a Tiffany ring box. Flicking it open, the diamond blinds me for a moment.)
Him: Marry me, Tess. Be mine forever.
Me: Put that 1.2 million dollar ring back in your pocket. We're not meant to be together. I must go.
Him: Wait! Tess! (He bursts into racking sobs.)
Me: (I wipe a tear as I head for the subway. My posture is excellent.)

Nice, huh? Okay, so here's what really happened.

Me: I don't think we can, I mean, uh, I don't think I can see you anymore.

Him: Okay.

Me: (pulling the knife from the center of my heart) Bye.

The first one's better. MUCH better, don't you think? Unfortunately, Brad, bless his pointed little head, didn't understand that he was losing a gem. That I am, indeed, one hell of a catch and he's a fool for letting me go.

Really. I mean that. Honest.

I love it, Erin, that you've been so lucky with your Man To Do. And I really mean that, too. I sit here and wonder where I went wrong. Dating dangerous, fabulously wealthy, terminally handsome boys seemed like a good idea at the time. What was a broken heart (or ten)? Nevertheless, I've learned my lesson. No more Men To Do... I'm doing Men To Marry now. Period. The end. Well, not the end so much as the beginning. A new beginning with a whole new me.

I'm going to do all the things Dear Abby suggests: church socials (note to self: find church), night classes (note to self: ditto), afternoon concerts in Central Park, maybe some golf lessons. I am determined to find Mr. Right and become Mrs. Right by the end of the year. Or next year. Soon, okay? No more Brads. Ever!

So don't you guys worry about me. You just crawl

into your respective beds with your respective hunks and don't give your poor, desperate friend a thought. I mean it.

Okay then. I'll just go cry myself to sleep. TTYS! Love and kisses,
Tess

1

DASH BLACK FINISHED his e-mail and sent it off, wishing he didn't have fifteen more to go. It would take hours, when all he wanted to do was lock himself in the music room and reacquaint himself with his piano.

Kelly, his assistant, was a godsend and handled his life with practiced ease, but she wasn't a magician. With the ever increasing success of Noir, he was just damn lucky he could work at home once in a blue moon. Given all the travel, public appearances and investor relations he'd had to do over the past year, sitting in his home office should have been reward enough, but he was a selfish bastard. He wanted it all. Most people would say that's just what he had. He said it to himself often enough. Like the prince who wants to see how the pauper lives, he had never rebelled, never known anything but his life of privilege. It was sick, the way he thought about it, when all he should be was grateful.

Screw it. Self-pity bored him even more than self-aggrandizement. Just do the work, and shut the hell—

"…the wonder dick. He wasn't even that good in bed, for heaven's sake."

Dash swiveled in his chair, but the startling feminine voice with the slight southern accent had come from outside. It wasn't Kelly's voice. Today was his housekeeper's day off. It was, damn, what was her name? The plant lady. Teresa, Toni? Tess. That's right. Tess. Tall, curvy, lips like Angelina Jolie. Somewhere in the back of his mind he'd known she came to his place to tend his plants, but he'd only seen her a couple of times. Which was a damn shame. He'd thought about those curves, and how they'd feel in his arms. Maybe he'd find out.

He sure as hell hoped she was talking on the phone, and not to an invisible "friend." In any case, he doubted she knew he was here, or she would have been a lot more discreet.

"Erin, I'm not rationalizing. Well, maybe I am, but I can't help it. This weekend is the most important of my life. Cullen is expecting me there, and if he comes through, I'll be able to put down the deposit on the store. I can't hang in limbo like this. It's now or never."

He shouldn't listen. This was obviously private. Especially that "wonder dick" comment.

"Okay, yes, I understand that it's a sign of immaturity to want to show up Brad and Lacey, but I don't care. I need someone spectacular on my arm and I'm running out of time. The party is Saturday night."

Dash frowned. Cullen? Could she mean Jim Cullen? He was a venture capitalist with a powerful track record. And he was going to the Hamptons this weekend for a party at Rain Nickleby's.

Her laughter drew him back to her conversation, his curiosity piqued even further. Were they both going to the same party? It would make sense. He'd seen

Tess at social functions before. She worked for a lot of influential people.

"...the mice are sewing up my dress right now, and the pumpkin is reserved. Now all I need is Prince Charming, and I'll be the belle of the ball."

He grinned. With her body, if he remembered correctly, she shouldn't have any trouble finding her prince, even if it was just for the night.

"And if I don't find Prince Charming, I'll settle for a rent-a-stud. Oh, God. Do you think they expect sex? I mean, is he going to be put out if I don't put out?"

Rent-a-stud? Dash stood and moved closer to the door.

"Yeah, like I've paid for escorts a hundred times before. Come on, Erin, I'm desperate here."

It occurred to Dash that this might be an interesting situation. If she was referring to the same party. He was no prince, but he also didn't charge for his services. No, that wouldn't work. His attendance wouldn't be for pleasure. He'd have to work the party, and what that required was someone useful on his arm.

She laughed again, a rich, throaty, uninhibited sound. He smiled. Screw it. When was the last time he'd had anonymous sex? Jeez, he couldn't remember. And when was the last time he'd had a woman who wasn't connected to Noir? Being a celebrity was great if you wanted a nice table, but it sucked if you wanted a one-night stand.

He walked into the hallway, wondering if he should cough or something so Tess wouldn't get scared. He rounded the corner to the living room, and there she was. At least part of her.

He had an exceptional view of her backside. And a nice backside it was. She was tending a plant, doing something with a bag of soil. If he coughed now, she'd be embarrassed. But if she stood up and saw him, she'd be scared. Which would be more to his advantage?

As he debated his next move, his gaze never wavered from the tantalizing view in front of him. Her jeans fit snugly over very voluptuous hips. He didn't see enough curves in his life. Even the models who posed for Noir were so damn skinny he kept wanting to cook them pasta. He'd never admit it, but the women in his magazine weren't exactly his taste. Heresy, but what can you do? He liked a woman who looked real. Shapely. Someone he could hold on to.

"Oh, right," she said.

She must have a headset on, because both hands were busy.

"Yeah, I'm sure he's dying to take me out. I haunt his dreams. Did you see last week's *People?* He was with Nicole Kidman, for God's sake."

Nicole… She was talking about him. He'd taken Nic to a premier, a charity event. This was getting more interesting by the moment.

"Don't I know it. He's so gorgeous. Just being here makes me wet."

Dash grinned. This was too easy. Like taking candy from a baby.

"Erin, you wicked creature. And here you try to pass yourself off as so nice. I know better, woman. You're evil. And I love that about you."

He wanted to know what Erin had said. He had the feeling he would have liked it a lot. Tess reached for more potting soil and he held his breath, certain she was going to see him. But she didn't. She did, however, crouch down. Damn. He'd better get the hell out of—

"Oh!" Tess jumped up, turned to face him, flinging dirt in all directions. Her horrified expression gave him a twinge of guilt.

"What are you...? When did you...? Oh, God."

"I'm sorry. I didn't mean to startle you."

"Startle me? I'm in the middle of a coronary, here. You shouldn't do that to people."

"I didn't realize you were here. I would have announced myself."

"A cough would have been fine. Oh, Jesus."

She put her hand over her heart, and his gaze moved down with it. Curves. Lush, touchable curves.

"What?"

He looked up at her, but she wasn't talking to him. There was the earpiece, the wires leading to a pocket on her apron.

"I gotta go," she said. "I'll explain later."

She reached into her pocket, then took the headset off. Her short, dark hair was in disarray, spiky and wild. He hadn't noticed how blue her eyes were but he sure as hell remembered that mouth. Damn, but he'd like to see those lips wrapped around his cock.

"You're home," she said.

"Yes, I am. I didn't mean to frighten you."

"But you're never home."

She sounded so shocked, he had to smile. "I come here from time to time."

"Oh."

"Why don't we go to the kitchen. You can get cleaned up."

She looked down at her hands, her short nails darkened by dirt, then her gaze went to the carpet. "Oops."

"It's fine." He nodded toward the other room. "Come on."

She swallowed, blinked, then let out a big breath. "Am I in trouble?"

"From what I could hear, I'd say so."

The panicked look came back to her face. "You heard me?"

He nodded. "We need to talk," he said as he headed for the kitchen, but he caught her whispered, "Oh, shit."

It wasn't nice, his little game. He should be ashamed of himself. Should be, but wasn't. Once in the kitchen, he got busy making some coffee. He'd have opened a bottle of wine, but it was a bit early in the day for that. After grinding the beans he measured the grounds, then added the water, and still, Tess hadn't come in. He was tempted to check on her, but decided to let her have some time to gather herself. So he just brought down two cups and sat at the table.

She came in a moment later, looking as scared as she was embarrassed.

"How do you like your coffee?"

Her brows came down as she studied him. "Do you always serve coffee to people before you fire them?"

"Who said I was going to fire you?"

Her relief lasted only a moment. A slight sigh, then

she shook her head and stared at him through narrowed eyes. "Then what was all that about me being in trouble."

"The party this weekend. You don't have a date."

"Excuse me?"

"Wash up while I pour," he said.

A brief glance at her hands spurred her over to the sink. As she scrubbed her hands and nails, she kept looking at him, puzzled as hell.

He brought out cream and sugar, a couple of spoons, then sat down at the table, bringing the carafe with him. A moment later, she sat across from him, her confusion making her eyes sparkle.

"I have a proposition for you," he said, enjoying the play of emotion on her face. Nothing was hidden in this one. She was an open book. Which could be dangerous in a town like Manhattan.

"What kind of proposition?"

"You're going to Rain Nickleby's this Saturday, right?"

She nodded.

"So am I." He poured the steaming coffee into her mug, but she didn't touch it. She did, however, clutch her spoon like a lifeline.

"And?"

"I don't have a date. I was hoping you'd be kind enough to accompany me."

She blinked several times. A sound came out of her, something between a gasp and a squeak. He tried hard not to look too smug.

"Are you kidding?"

"Not at all. You'd be doing me a great favor."

"*I'd* be doing *you* a favor."

"You would. Up until an hour ago, I wasn't looking forward to the party, and now I am."

She blinked again. Her long, dark lashes splashed against her pale skin. Soft skin. "I thought you were dating Nicole Kidman."

"No. We're not dating. Our evenings out have been strictly business."

"Gee, that must be so rough."

He laughed. "With Nic, it's not rough. But that's not always the case. Sometimes it's pretty hard pasting a smile on."

She sat back in her chair, her T-shirt snug around her breasts. Abundant, full breasts. Her whole body was ample and curvaceous, and he felt the familiar pull at his groin. He hadn't wanted to go to the party at all. Now, he could hardly wait.

"Why?" she asked.

"Why, what?"

"Why would you want to take me?"

"Why not?"

"I water your plants."

"Yes, you do."

"I'm no Nicole Kidman."

"No, you're not. You're Tess, and I'd be honored to have you be my date. I'll pick you up at five on Saturday. It'll take us a while to get out to the island."

She sighed again, then nibbled a bit on her lower lip. He averted his gaze, finally taking a drink of his coffee. It had been a long time since he'd had this kind of reaction to a woman. Not that he was immune to the considerable charms of the ladies he met through Noir, but this was something unrehearsed. A surprise in a world that held very few. Whatever happened Saturday night, it would keep him on his toes. Which appealed greatly.

"I don't understand it," she said, "but I'd be a total loon to say no."

He grinned. "Good, then. It's settled."

"I suppose you heard why I'm going?"

"I know Cullen. He's very savvy, and he makes most of his business decisions based on his reaction to the person, not the proposal. I think you'll do very well."

"Really?"

"You'll have to tell me about your plans on the way to the party. Unfortunately, I have to get back to work."

She stood up quickly, a splash of pink coloring her cheeks. "I really appreciate this, Mr. Black."

"Dash."

"Right."

He stood next to her, took her hand in his, felt her tremble. Her scent, subtle, slightly citrus, made him want to touch far more. "I appreciate this. More than you can know."

She looked down at her feet, then brought her gaze up to meet his. "I think you have that backward."

"Five o'clock, Tess."

"Do you know where I live?"

"I'll find you."

"Maybe I should just meet you here."

He shook his head slowly. "I'll find you."

She swallowed. Blinked in that way she had. "I'll be ready."

He kissed the back of her hand, instantly registering that he'd been right about the softness of her skin. He didn't particularly want to let her go, but he did. "Until then."

"Uh-huh," she whispered, looking a little dazed.

"You okay?"

"Oh, sure. No big deal. So what if you're Dash Black. Frankly, I'm a little bored with it already."

He laughed. "We're going to have us a good time, Tess."

She shook her head. "I think maybe you're a little crazy."

"A little."

"Cool."

He took a step toward his office, then turned back and kissed her cheek. Mostly because he'd wanted another hit of her scent. He'd expected her to smell like flowers, and she'd surprised him. Her blush was an added bonus. So was the spark of mischief in her eyes.

"Uh, Dash?"

"Yes?"

"I'm not really bored."

"Cool," he said back, liking the feel of the word almost as much as her pleased reaction. No, boredom wasn't going to enter into this at all.

Tess HAD NO IDEA HOW LONG she'd stood in his kitchen after he'd left. It was still daylight, which was a good thing. She had to clean up her mess in the other room, and finish the plants. But her whole mind, hell, her whole being, was totally transfixed by one thing.

She was going on a date with Dashiell Black.

The most gorgeous man she'd ever seen in print or in life. She knew more about him than she should. That he was six foot three, that he had a passion for music. She could verify the first fact, but the music thing was something she'd read in the *Enquirer*. She'd also read that he'd had an illicit affaire with an ex-first lady, but come on. One thing she didn't get from reading the tabloids was that luscious, slightly spicy scent of his. Or the way his hazel eyes snapped with amusement.

And he was taking her, Tess Norton of Tulip, Texas, to a party in the Hamptons. How could she think of anything else? This was huge. This was monumental. This was going to give her a heart attack. What was she going to wear? She had no shoes! *Hair.* Her hair looked like someone chopped it off with a bread knife.

Oh, God. Dash Black. It had taken her months to get over the fact that she worked for the man. Every time she'd seen him, she'd practically swooned. *Swooned.* He was…

Perfect.

And she was…

Tess.

Oh, God.

2

TESS STOOD IN THE MIDDLE of Rags to Riches, her favorite resale shop, holding a vintage Chanel when it hit her again. In two days, she was going on a date with Dash.

Dash Black. Who made her legs turn to jelly, her heart palpitate, her mind go blank. It wasn't just that he was famous. In her years in Manhattan, she'd met lots of famous people. Everyone from Robert De Niro to Trent Reznor. She'd been lucky. One of the first people she'd met in the city was an interior designer to the stars. Shelly had unbelievable contacts, and when Tess started her plant-care business, Shelly had used her influence to introduce Tess to the A-list.

At first, it had been overwhelming. Scary. She'd been intimidated and shy, which wasn't her natural state of being. But walking into the luxurious penthouses of the incredibly rich and famous was enough to turn her into a little mouse.

Eventually, as she became more relaxed, she began to see the similarities instead of the differences. Even Academy Award winners had bathrooms.

Then, when Cole Darden of daytime drama fame had asked her out, she'd been introduced into yet another strata. The club scene. Not the clubs she would have been able to get into. These clubs had bouncers that made a hundred grand a year. It was heady and wild and she found herself knee-deep in celebrity gossip that never made the *Post*.

The downside was that she wasn't in a financial position to be a player. It wasn't the drinks or the dinners or the tips. She didn't drink much, and her dates usually paid for the rest. It was the clothes. Damn those women on *Sex and the City*. They had to be millionaires to afford those wardrobes. Unfortunately for Tess, she didn't have a studio behind her, and she sure as hell couldn't pay for a Prada scarf. So it was resale shops, Goodwill, flea markets for her. It stretched her creativity, that's for sure. But it also made her terribly aware that while she was allowed inside, she'd better not get too comfortable. She was on a guest pass, which could be revoked in ten hot seconds.

Not a good train of thought, given her situation. She still couldn't figure out why he'd asked her to go with him. Pity, probably.

She could handle that.

She went back to the rack of dresses, most of which were here for a reason. Every once in a while, however, she found a gem. Please, let it be today. So much was riding on this one Saturday night, not the least of which was showing Brad that she didn't miss him at all. That other men, fabulous men, wanted her.

Well, maybe not wanted her, but Brad didn't have to know that. Dash would treat her like a queen. Because that's how he treated every woman. She just prayed she wouldn't turn into a frog. Do something stupid, say the wrong thing, act like a fool. Her usual.

"Well, if it isn't fabulous Tess Norton."

Tess grinned at the haughty voice behind her. It was Mary, her friend, neighbor, partner in crime. She turned and waggled her brows. "Mary Neal. I never."

"Like hell, you never."

"Such language."

"I'm not even warmed up yet."

Tess eyed Mary's outfit du jour. Doc Martens, jeans that rode low on her impossibly slim hips, a sweater circa the 1960s, and a furry coat that might have belonged to Attila the Hun. On her, it worked. "I'm desperate, girlfriend."

"Tell Aunt Mary all about it."

The store, close packed, a little too warm, was one of their usual haunts, not just for the occasional finds, but because there was this great coffee shop next door that served the best apple strudel in the universe.

"I will. In aching detail. But first, I need something fabulous. Something transcendent. Something that will give every male above eighteen an instant erection."

Mary glanced at the dress in her hand. "That won't even get you a slap on the ass." She spread the clothes on the rack like Moses parting the sea. "Let's rock."

Two hours later, after having tried on everything from Versace to Polo, Tess cried uncle. She grabbed Mary's hand and pulled her outside into the balmy spring air. Her gaze moved automatically toward the downtown skyline, and, as always, her breath hitched when she saw what was missing. Turning back to Mary, who had pulled out a compact and was busy dusting her perfect little nose, Tess pointed to the café, with the improbable name of Frog and Thistle. "Food. Now."

"Okay. Jeez." Mary slipped the cloisonné powder case into her Kate Spade pocketbook, then smiled. "But you have to tell me what this mad search is all about."

"I will. Come on," she said, dodging a guy on a skateboard as she headed toward the Frog. "I have to find a dress today. Tomorrow, latest. I need it by Saturday night."

"Don't keep me waiting. It's mean."

Tess slipped inside the café and told the scrumptious young man at the counter that she wanted a table for two. She followed his tightly clad butt across the crowded restaurant, past the tables with their gingham cloths and fresh carnations, to a snug booth in the back. Mary shrugged out of her coat, then sat down. "Well?"

"Okay, okay. No need to get all huffy."

"Tess…"

Tess didn't smile. She was pretty sure she didn't look smug. And she kept her voice low, so only Mary would hear. "I have a date with Dash Black."

Mary screamed so loudly a waiter dropped his tray, all chatter came to an immediate stop, and every eye in the place zeroed in on their booth. Mary finally closed her mouth, then seemed to realize they were the center of attention. She turned to the stunned restaurant patrons. "She has a date with Dash Black."

Tess couldn't hold back her grin as she saw utter understanding come over the mostly female crowd. Several women nodded. More than a few stared at her with awe. He was, after all, Dash Black. And he was hers, hers, hers for one whole night.

She felt like she might throw up.

WHEN DASH WALKED INTO HIS brother's office, Patrick was already studying the glossy photos spread out before him. His expression was serious, his focus sharp. It was time to pick the September centerfold. Dash had made his choice. Although a whole editorial team helped narrow the field, the family—himself, Patrick and their father—had the final word.

Dash headed over to Patrick's bookshelves and gave them a cursory glance. The only new entries were a James Patterson book, a biography of Napoleon, and the latest bestseller on business communication. Slim pickings.

With nothing to keep him occupied, he gave in and settled himself on one of Patrick's leather chairs. Sprawled with legs out, he waited for his half brother to look at him, but clearly Patrick wasn't going to budge until he was damn good and ready.

The office was too similar to his own to be of interest. Lots of square footage decorated in masculine colors, mostly hunter green, with bits and pieces of their various enterprises represented in knickknacks, photographs, logo promotions, and, inevitably, stacks of the magazine.

Noir's circulation was at an all-time high. Millions of men bought the magazine each month, and some of them probably read the articles. His father had set out to make *Noir* a household name, and he'd succeeded beyond his wildest dreams. In the old days, Black had been the front man. Suave, sophisticated, charming as hell, he'd been the driving force behind Noir, but he was done now. Tired. He had every right to be. He'd worked his ass off most of his life. Dash had been his ace in the hole. He could hand over the keys to the kingdom with little fear. With every expectation that their success would continue, that the companies would grow. That Dash would be as enthusiastic and tireless as his father.

The flesh was willing, but the mind was weak. Dash stared at his future with a kind of stunned resolve. The world on a string, and he didn't like yo-yos. He'd better damn well get to like yo-yos. There was no way he was going to spend the next thirty years dissatisfied and resentful.

Actually, that wasn't fair. It's not that he hated running the show, he simply wasn't his father. Dash was a private man thrust into the spotlight. He envied Patrick, with his focus on the real guts of the operation. The money.

Dash jumped a bit when he realized he was staring at Patrick, and that his brother was staring back. "How long have you been watching me?"

Pat shrugged. "Long enough to wonder what's bothering you."

Dash waved a dismissive hand. "Nothing a lobotomy wouldn't fix."

"Ah, well. We do have that excellent health insurance plan. I'm sure we could work something out."

"Gee, thanks."

"Come on, Dash. What's up?"

"I like Marie, what's her last name? Clymer? The redhead on the second row."

Patrick looked at his proofs. "Yeah, that's who I

was leaning toward, but don't change the subject. What's wrong?"

"Nothing."

Patrick's right brow arched. "Fine. Have it your way. Why did you come to see me?"

"I'm going to that party in the Hamptons this weekend. I was thinking we should send a photographer out."

"To the Nicklebys' place?"

Dash nodded.

"Already taken care of."

Now it was Dash's turn to raise his eyebrow. "Efficient little sucker, aren't you?"

"I strive for excellence in all areas."

Dash gave him the old raspberry. "Excellence, my ass."

"No wonder you're the heir apparent," Patrick said. "Your maturity and class are a shining example to all."

Dash stood up, stretched his neck. "Hey, you know the plant lady?"

"Tess?"

He nodded. "Yeah. I'm taking her."

"To the party?"

"Yeah."

"Why?"

"Because she needs a date, and I'm a goddamn prince of a fellow." Dash headed for the door.

"Wait a minute. I don't like it."

He stopped. "Don't like what?"

"She's a nice girl, Dash. And she's an employee."

"So?"

"It's not a good idea, that's all."

"What do you mean?"

Patrick shuffled some photos. "You know perfectly well what I mean. She's not a toy."

Dash went over to the edge of Patrick's teak desk. He leaned forward, balancing on his flattened palms. "Are you interested in her?"

Patrick's gaze shot to his. "No. I'm not. But I like her. She's bright and ambitious, but she's also young as hell, and she comes from the middle of nowhere. So don't set her up for a fall. That's all I'm saying."

"I'm taking her to a party, Patrick. Not to a wedding."

"Yeah, well, women tend to fall in love with you. God knows why."

"Yeah, I love you, too." He straightened, fully aware Patrick was dead-on serious. "I'll be good," he said. "I promise."

"Why aren't I taking comfort from that statement?"

Dash shook his head as if he had no idea.

"Oh, get the hell out of my office. Some of us have to work for a living."

Dash decided to let Patrick have the last word. He nodded once, then headed in the direction of his own office. His brother didn't usually stick his nose in Dash's business. It made Dash all the more intrigued with Tess. She had clearly made an impression on someone who wasn't that impressionable.

Based on their history, Dash believed Patrick about not being interested in Tess, but still, there was some connection there. The two of them had clearly talked, which made sense. It was Patrick who'd originally hired her to do the plant maintenance in the Midtown offices. What was it about her that made his brother so protective?

Actually, what was it that made Dash so hot to trot? Maybe he shouldn't have been so flippant with Patrick. Tess was a damsel in distress, and he was playing the role of knight. It wasn't a good fit. He normally played the rake.

But for one night? Why not. He could be Lochinvar. Hell, most of his public life was all an act anyway. It would be a change of pace, and that was a plus. He remembered her curves, the way her breasts had looked in that T-shirt. Pity. But everything in life wasn't sex. It only felt that way.

RED, ANKLE LENGTH, NO LABEL, no mars in the luxurious silk, fifty dollars. The dress was a gift from kind gods, and fit her as if designed with her in mind. Fifty dollars. Tess grinned madly as she paid the woman with the bad teeth, then hugged her package close as she made her way out of the small resale shop.

Tomorrow was the big day. Dash Black day. His secretary, Kelly, had called that morning to make all the arrangements. The car, which Tess knew was actually a limousine, would be at her apartment shortly after five. The drive to Amagansett took about three hours, what with the tolls and the traffic.

Three hours alone with *him*.

What would they talk about? Would they have champagne? Champagne gave her a headache. She'd suffer.

Dammit, she had to calm down. This wasn't a real date. It was a mercy date, and she'd better remember it. Right. As if she hadn't been writing, "Mrs. Dashiell Black" and "Mrs. Tess Black" on every napkin from the Brooklyn Deli to Capizio's Pizza by the Slice. Mature, Tess. Real mature.

She made her way across Christopher Street, blinking into the late afternoon glare. She had major girly stuff to do tonight. Mud mask, fingernails, toenails, plucking, shaving, waxing. The fun never ends. Maybe Mary would come by. Or maybe Tess would just drown herself in her bathtub.

She walked two long blocks, forcing herself to ignore the three shoe store displays, staring, instead, directly in front of her. She didn't have money for shoes. She'd wear her black strappy heels. So they were almost two years old. Who was going to look at her feet?

God, the dress! It caressed her curves...not her words; the lady with the teeth had been eloquent. But it was a knockout. And she felt pretty in it, which was even more important.

Why was it that she could be so self-assured about her business and her plans, but when it came to her private life her insecurities had insecurities? It didn't seem fair. She wasn't the rube from Texas anymore. She'd lived in the big, bad city long enough to have been mugged, evicted and dumped by some very high-class guys. Dash Black should be just another fascinating peek at New York, like the Rainbow Room or the bag ladies outside Central Park.

Uh-huh.

She got bumped twice on her way down the stairs to the subway, and some great galoot nearly crippled her when he stepped on her toe, but she made it to the train, and even got a seat, although she had to sit next to someone who used garlic as aftershave.

The ride was only twenty minutes to her stop, and then she'd have a quick five minute walk. She would stop at the market on the corner and pick up some salad for dinner.

Dash Black.

It had become her mantra. And like women who couldn't get pregnant and saw babies everywhere, Tess had been deluged with pictures of her dream date.

He'd been on the cover of *Esquire* wearing the most scrumptious charcoal-gray shirt. The color made his hazel eyes look blue. His smile had been sly, as if he knew a secret, and maybe he'd tell her what it was.

He'd also been in *Vogue, Cosmo, Mademoiselle* and the *National Enquirer.* Not that she read that…she'd just been killing time in the checkout line.

Every picture had been beautiful, and she'd pasted each one, except for the tabloid, in a brand new scrapbook she kept hidden under her bed. It might look naive to save his pictures, but she'd be glad in twenty years when she wanted to show her grandchildren that granny had been a hottie.

Besides, she liked looking at him. His wide shoulders and slim hips. His dark hair that fell ever so provocatively across his forehead. That nose! Mary said it was big, and maybe it was, but it was strong and had much more character than one of the waspier models. And then, oh my, there were the lips. The bottom one in particular. Pouty, lush, perfect but not fem. Designed for kissing. The thought of that mouth on hers...

She shivered, and got a glare from Garlic Man.

Ignoring him, she opened her bag and took out her to-do list. Yep, she had everything she'd need. Sunday, she had to go to the flower mart, Monday, she'd start the new account over at Trump Plaza, and Tuesday was Eve's Apple night, so she had to finish reading *The Pearl,* which she hadn't even opened yet, but for tonight, she was good to go. She'd listen to some Linkin Park and maybe some Creed. Throw in a little Joni Mitchell for flavor. She even had that bottle of Merlot Brad had given her after he'd stood her up for the second night in a row. But that was then. This was now and tonight was going to be wonderful as long as she didn't dwell on tomorrow. As long as her nerves held steady and her tummy didn't go nuts. As long as she could pretend it was like any other night in a perfectly ordinary universe.

Uh-huh.

3

DASH CLIMBED TO THE second floor of the old brownstone, then looked at his watch. It was four-fifty. He wondered how far along Tess was in getting ready. Experience had shown him that women were genetically predisposed to lateness connected in any way with makeup or hair products. So, he'd wait. He just hoped the limo would be safe downstairs. The neighborhood left something to be desired.

He walked up two more flights of stairs trying to ignore a scent he didn't want to think about, then down a murky hallway. Three lights had burned out. Tess should ask the landlord to fix them. It wasn't safe. Anyone could hide in one of the shadowy doorways.

Then he found apartment 42. He knocked, straightened his bow tie, pulled his tux jacket down in back, and with some effort, relaxed. He'd mention the light situation casually, while she was puttering around with her last-minute touches. He wouldn't say a word about the smell.

When the door swung open, his hello caught as a strange woman smiled at him.

"I'm looking for Tess?"

The woman, thin, attractive with her large eyes and

button nose, stepped back to let him in. "Tess is almost ready," she said. "I'm Mary, her neighbor."

"Nice to meet you, Mary." He took her hand in his and kissed the back. Women liked that. Mary's grin confirmed a direct hit. "I'm Dash Black."

"Yeah. I kinda figured."

He smiled, hiding his surprise at her interesting wardrobe choices. A Scooby-Doo T-shirt over a pair of jeans so large she could fit in them twice, held up by red suspenders. Her hair was seminormal, if you considered a streak of purple normal.

"You want something to drink?" Mary shut the door. "There's some Merlot that's pretty decent."

"No, thank you. There's going to be enough of that at the party."

Mary led him into a small living room. Really small. Dash hadn't been in an apartment like this in years. He'd forgotten people actually lived like this. Typical in Manhattan, it would be considered a shoe closet in most other cities. There was room for a love seat, a chair, a lamp and a coffee table of sorts. When he looked closer, he saw it was a tree stump with a glass top.

"Have a seat." Mary plopped down on the chair, so Dash took the love seat. He sank into it until his knees were above his waist. Getting up wasn't going to be easy. He prayed Tess was almost ready.

"So, what's it like being you?"

He looked sharply at the Scooby-Doo woman. "I don't know. I haven't given it much thought."

"Are you happy?"

Who was this strange girl? She looked to be in her mid-twenties, and from what he could see she didn't have a speck of makeup on her squeaky clean face. "For the most part."

"Hmm," she said, sounding too much like a therapist for his taste.

"What?"

"I've only seen you smiling. In magazines, and stuff. So I guess I've just thought of you as happy all the time."

"No one's happy all the time."

"Yeah, but—"

"Mary, stop bugging the nice man."

Tess's voice came from the doorway behind him, and using his hand on the frame for leverage, Dash stood, relieved as hell. He wanted out of here, to be on his own turf. He turned, then stopped dead still. Tess was a vision of luscious womanhood in a red dress that made his throat dry. Her hair looked wild, like she'd just gotten well and lustily laid, and her eyes were luminous with mischief and something else he couldn't peg. But where he got stuck was her lips.

Red, like the dress, full, like her breasts. He wanted to pull her to him, feel that body from shoulder to knee, and kiss her senseless.

"Please excuse my friend," Tess said, walking toward him with a sinful sway of hips. "We normally don't let her speak to strangers unless she's taken her Prozac."

He smiled as he caught Mary's surreptitious one-finger salute. But his attention was on Tess. Only Tess. "You look stunning."

She lowered her lashes as her cheeks pinked. "Thank you." Shyly, she looked at him again, her gaze moving down his tuxedo, then back up. "So do you."

He laughed. "Stunning? I don't think so."

Her head tilted to the side. "You are."

He waved away the compliment, and took hold of her hand. This time, when he kissed the delicate skin on the back, he lingered, inhaling deeply her sweet honey scent. "The coach awaits," he said, reluctant to let go of her.

"I just need my bag."

Her hand was lost to him, but in recompense, he got to watch as she walked to the tiny kitchen to collect her purse. The curves were just as impressive from this side.

He tried to remember why he'd decided to keep his hands off Tess. Patrick's face came to mind. For about two seconds. He took one more look at Tess's backside and banished his brother for the night.

"Okay, I'm all set," she said.

He crossed the room in three strides and captured her hand once more. "It's going to be a great party," he said as he led her toward the front door. "And I'm going to be the luckiest man there."

Tess faced him with a frown. "Maybe you should take Mary. You two have a lot in common."

"What do you mean?"

"You'd understand if you knew her."

He nodded at the woman still curled up in the chair. "While I'd be delighted to get to know you better, tonight is for Tess."

"Be good," Mary said. "And if you can't be good, be safe. Remember, no glove, no love."

"Mary?" Tess said sweetly.

"Yes?"

"Remind me to kill you when I get home, okay?"

"I'll leave you a note." She waved all five fingers this time. "Have fun, kids."

Dash got the door, and once he and Tess were in the hallway, his gaze went right to a burned-out bulb. "This isn't safe," he said. "You need those lights fixed. You don't even have a doorman."

"I know," she said. "But I've come to the conclusion that the super here is a hologram."

"Then you should contact the landlord."

"I'll do my best."

"Promise?"

She nodded. "It's okay. Honest. Thanks for your concern."

"Well, it's dangerous."

"So is walking in these heels."

He got the hint and led her down all the stairs to the street. Some kid had his boom box on painful-death-bass, and some other kid was screaming up to his mother on the fifth floor, but the limo was still intact, the engine purring, waiting for them.

Moe, Dash's driver for over five years, smiled as he opened the back door. Moe was forty-seven, with a shocking thatch of thick black hair and a mustache to match. He didn't look it, but he was also a bodyguard. His CIA training had been supplemented by years mastering karate.

"Good evening, ma'am. Let me help you into that seat. The step is a little tricky."

Tess thanked him while Dash went to the other door. A moment later, they were happily settled in the quiet of the car. "Get comfortable," he said. "It's three hours."

"I could run up and get my bunny slippers."

"Or I could pour you a cocktail."

"Bunny slippers are highly overrated."

The limo was well stocked, and after a moment of concentration, Tess decided on an apple martini. Dash got the shaker, the ice and the vodka, but he almost dumped the whole thing in his lap. Inattention. She'd leaned back, taken a deep breath, and he was all thumbs. It wasn't like him. He disconcerted women, not the other way around. Pulling himself together, he poured her drink, fixed himself a scotch and water, then leaned back next to her. Not close enough.

She sipped, moaned with pleasure, then sighed. He felt inordinately pleased.

"I can see why Mary asked you those questions," she said softly.

It took him a moment to remember. "About being happy?"

Tess nodded. "It's tricky when you only see a public image. I don't know you at all."

"Why don't we fix that."

"Right. Three hours."

"Ask 'em if you've got 'em. If, that is, I get to ask you questions in return."

"My life's an open book. I wish I had skeletons in the closet, but so far, it's only dust bunnies."

"I see a motif shaping up here. Did you have bunnies as a child? Did you have an issue with a bunny?"

She laughed, throaty, rich. "Nary a bunny crossed my path. It's Mary's influence, I'm convinced. Being around her too long would make anyone a little nuts, and she's my best friend.''

"I'll wager you have lots of friends."

She sipped her drink, then put the glass down between them on the leather seat. "I have enough. I grew up in a very small town, and so I had a gang there. Mostly out of self-defense. The boredom factor was daunting. One movie theater. No mall. It wasn't pretty.''

"And now?''

"New York isn't exactly the easiest place to make friends, but I have a few. Mary. The woman who brought me into the plant business. My online girl-friends, of course. And Tate.'' At the name, her face softened.

"And who would Tate be?''

"He's a wonderful man who takes me to the the-ater.''

"Oh?''

"No, it's not like that. He'd old enough to be my father. He's someone special, though. I'm glad I know him.''

"What makes him special?''

She shrugged her shoulders, reminding him again of her proximity and his hormones. "He's incredibly passionate about what he loves, and he shares that with me. There are no compromises in Tate.''

"It's a lucky man who doesn't have to compro-mise.''

"I'm not sure it's about luck. I think, in his case, he simply was prepared to pay the price.''

Dash brought his glass up to his lips and savored the aged scotch as it heated a trail down his throat.

Some compromises were harder than others, that's all. She didn't know that yet. She was so young.

Tess felt the change in him, although she had no idea what had caused it. One moment she was dizzy in the focus of Dash's scrutiny, and then she'd lost him. She'd only been talking about Tate...

Oh, God. Maybe that was it. He'd assumed she'd told him about Tate so he would know the coast was clear. But this wasn't a real date, and he wasn't really interested, just polite.

Maybe, if she could pretend to be as smooth and confident as she sounded, she wouldn't feel like throwing up. She'd had the gift always. No one ever saw her sweat or shake or fumble for words. Which didn't mean she wasn't quaking inside.

The black stretch limo, complete with uniformed chauffer, the red dress, Dash...who wouldn't be a complete wreck? God, but he was gorgeous. The tuxedo was something out of a James Bond movie, and Dash was made to wear it. He was the ultimate playboy, the elegant scoundrel who broke hearts as easily as she broke her nails.

At the thought, she looked down at her hands. The press-on nails were still attached, shiny with red polish to match her dress. No one would guess she really had gardener's fingernails, so short they didn't even reach the tip of her fingers.

Her gaze went back to Dash, to his expression. The frown line between his brows had gone, and he looked back at her with real interest. "What?"

"I was just thinking," he said.

"About?"

"Your business proposal."

Her stomach clenched and she almost dropped her drink. "Thanks a lot. I'd managed to put that terror on hold for a while."

"Sorry, although I don't see what you have to be afraid of. Cullen is going to love you."

"From your lips…"

He grinned, and she felt it down to her toes. Perfect teeth, that bottom lip. Oh, my.

"Don't sweat it. I mean it. What had me puzzled was why you didn't approach me."

"For what?"

"For the funding."

"Why would I do that?"

"For the same reason every other entrepreneur in the city does. Because I could help."

"I work for you. This is separate."

"It never occurred to you?"

"No. Don't look at me that way. I'm serious."

"I believe you."

"Okay, then." She finished off her martini, then handed him the empty glass. "I did want to say again how much this means to me. It's way over and above the call of duty. You're helping me big time."

"No thanks necessary. I'm getting as much out of this as you are."

"Which is something I don't fully understand."

"Not much to understand. I get to escort a beautiful lady to a party."

"Yeah, uh-huh."

His grin turned a little sheepish. "Okay, so there's a bit more. All those pictures you see of me smiling? That's work. And it's not easy work. Not that I'm complaining. I know I'm the luckiest sonofabitch in the world, but still. It's not easy to be happy twenty-four-seven.''

"So you don't have to work tonight?''

"Not in the same way. If I was with, say, an actress or a model, there would be speculation, constant photos, questions, innuendoes. With you, they'll be curious, of course, but not rabid.''

"So I'm not going to appear on the cover of *People?*''

"Most likely not,'' he said. "Are you disappointed?''

"Crushed.''

His grin faded. "I—''

She touched his arm. "I was kidding. I'm very happy to be whatever you need me to be tonight. Honestly.''

His gaze moved down to his arm, where her hand touched his sleeve.

She knew she should take it back, let him go, but she felt frozen. It was absurd, but she could swear she felt his heat. Impossible through shirt and coat. It hadn't started out as an intimate gesture, but it had turned into one. Stoked by his gaze, the heat spread through her. And still, she didn't move her hand.

"That could get a little tricky,'' he said, his voice lower, huskier than just a moment before.

"What could?''

"You being whatever I need you to be.''

"Oh.''

He leaned toward her and she held her breathe. He was going to kiss her. Oh, God. But he stopped short, inches away from her lips. His breath, a ridiculously intoxicating blend of scotch and spearmint, slipped inside her. "Very tricky," he whispered. And then his lips touched hers.

Before she could even close her eyes, he was gone. She blinked, tried to remember how to breathe.

He cleared his throat. Tugged his cuffs down. Looked out the window, at the moon roof, at the bar. Finally, at her. His frown surprised her. "I'm sorry."

"For what?"

"There are no strings attached to this evening. I apologize."

"Don't worry on my account." She gasped the second the words were out of her mouth.

He laughed, but not at her. Not making fun. In fact, the sound made her feel a fraction less foolish. "Okay, so at least we know one thing."

"That I need to learn to keep my big mouth shut?"

"No. That we're both a little nervous about to-night."

"I can understand me, but not you."

"I'm always a little nervous around a beautiful woman."

She nearly made a smart remark, but something stopped her. His eyes, or maybe his hint of a smile. Something made her entertain the idea that he could be telling the truth. That he thought she was beautiful.

She wasn't a hag or anything, but please. She was just Tess. Ten pounds overweight, ugly nails, hair that looked like it was done in a blender. Not Nicole or Meg or Julia. She was a hick from Tulip, that's all. And he was the most sophisticated, debonair man on planet Earth.

Which, of course, explained it. He was working tonight. Despite his protests. He couldn't help it.

When you seduce women for a living, it must come naturally, like breathing or sleeping. So it would be wise not to let her imagination run away with her.

This wasn't a coach, he wasn't a prince, and she sure as hell wasn't Cinderella.

"Tess."

She focused on him with a start. She'd been far away in the land of insecurity. "Yes?"

"No matter the reason. Favor to you, favor to me. Whatever. I'm glad I'm here, now, with you."

She smiled as warmly as she could, but she wasn't fooled this time. He was the embodiment of a smooth operator. A man so suave he made Cary Grant seem like an oaf. Of course he was going to flatter her. "Thank you," she said. "I'm glad, too."

If ever there was a Man To Do, Dash Black was him. Never, not in a million years, would he become a Man To Marry. Not to her, at least. Never to her.

4

SHE DIDN'T ACTUALLY SEE the house for a long time.
The gate had come first, ornate wrought iron with an
incongruously hi-tech security box on the driver's
side. Then it was like riding through a park. An ex-
traordinarily well-kept park. Manicured lawns. A
rogue blade of grass wouldn't dare show up there, let
alone a weed. The trees, all native to this part of the
country, were stately and thick, providing ample
shade for their flowered skirts.

A full-time staff would be essential in keeping this
gorgeous lawn so pristine, and she wondered about
the budget. They probably spent a fortune on fresh
flowers and plants for the house, too. Whoever had
the account must be doing very well.

Dash shifted beside her, and her thoughts of plants
and bank accounts fled. He'd been quiet since the
kiss, in deference to her, she thought. Someone more
savvy would probably have played the moment better.
Teased him. Chastised him. But her famous aplomb
had deserted her, and no soothing thoughts or dis-
tractions could bring it back.

"Have you been out here before?"

She didn't jump when he spoke, and that was a
bonus. "No, I haven't. It's stunning."

"This house used to belong to one of the Duponts,'' he said. ''It's got twenty-two bedrooms, not counting the guest house.''

''Well, that's got to be a pain to vacuum.''

His laughter eased her somewhat. However, his proximity— They weren't touching. But there was only enough space between them for one hand. If she let hers fall, she'd touch him, and that wasn't smart.

She tried to think what her friends would do. Erin would tell her to wait. Samantha would tell her to go for it. Neither option felt right. There was a whole evening to get through, and she couldn't afford to fall apart. Cullen would be watching her. Not to mention Brad and the Bitch.

Lacey. What a piece of work. Her nose was so far in the air it was amazing she didn't constantly walk into walls. And that smile—

''Tess?''

She turned to Dash. Smiled. ''Yes?''

''Where did you go?''

''Actually, I was thinking about Lacey Talbot.''

His expression hardened, which made Tess like him even more. ''She's an interesting young woman.''

''That's one way of putting it.''

''Don't pay any attention to her,'' he said, as he leaned over to place his glass back in the bar. ''She has issues.''

Tess couldn't help but giggle. She hated to giggle. Hers was all girly, making her feel too young to handle her job let alone this date. Sort of date. Whatever.

''But I will warn you. The way you look tonight, you're going to set her on edge.''

''Me?''

"Yes, you. I told you before, you're stunning."

She held her breath for a moment, then let it out slowly. It didn't mean anything. How could it? But she steadied her gaze and said, "Thank you," just like her mother had taught her.

He looked at her quizzically, but said nothing, then his gaze moved forward and he nodded. "The palace."

She turned to see lights. Lots of lights. The house, which did actually remind her of a palace, was bathed in white, and the long trail of parking lights from the limos in front of them reminded her of a red carpet.

She'd never seen a home like this. If it was even called a home. Estate, maybe. Or mansion. By any other name it was huge and she felt every year of her Tulip, Texas, education bite her in the ass. This was a mistake.

"If we get separated inside, just set off a flare. I should find you in two or three days."

She smiled, although it didn't seem like much of a joke. "I can't imagine this. It's like going to the moon."

"Kay Nickleby has an eating disorder that's sent four shrinks back to the minors. Her daughter, Phoebe, is a card-carrying kleptomaniac who once tried to steal one of Princess Diana's tiaras. Not to mention William, who has been kicked out of every prep school on the east coast. Roger Nickleby is having his day with the SEC, and I expect he'll be spending a large part of his fortune before he's through."

"So, you're telling me it's better to be poor?"

He frowned. "Hell no. I'm saying wackos come in every tax bracket."

She had to smile. "What about you? Are you a wacko?"

He nodded. "Oh, yeah."

The limo slowed to a stately crawl as they inched up the drive. Doormen stood at the ready, offering steady hands to extravagantly dressed women as they stepped out of their coaches.

Tess's heart picked up its pace. She ran her fingers through her hair, then pulled her compact from her purse. After a brief dusting of translucent powder and a refresh with her lip gloss, she turned to Dash. "It's show time."

"Don't worry. You're going to knock 'em dead."

"Frankly, I'm more worried about tripping on the stairs."

He touched her hand. "I'll be there. Don't sweat it."

She nodded. "Okay."

Then her door swung open, and a dark hand helped her to the curb. Dash was at her side a few seconds later, and when she felt his arm curl around her waist, she felt her shoulders relax.

All relaxation fled as they approached the steps. A small cadre of photographers spread around them, the flashbulbs making her squint.

"Dash, over here."

"Who's the babe?"

"Smile."

The shouts were good-natured, but insistent, and she felt utterly out of her element. Dash's arm tightened around her but his body felt loose and easy. This wasn't a big deal to him, of course, and she tried to adopt his casual air. Unsuccessfully, as it turned out.

A photographer breached the tacit space agreement and popped up inches from her shoulder. "Hey, babe!"

When she turned, he snapped her picture, blinding her with the flash, and she stumbled on the step. Dash held on to her, although it was a near thing, and his hold tightened as he straightened her up. She couldn't see his face, but she felt him tense like a bow string. Their pace changed into a quick march past the reporters and past the reception line until they were safely inside. He didn't let her go, though.

"Are you all right?"

She nodded. The black dot that was her vision dimmed and his features came into focus. "That was interesting."

"Whoever that jackass was, he's not going to be around for long. I'm sorry that had to happen to you."

"It's okay. He just scared me a little. I'm fine."

"You're not fine." He relaxed a bit as he smiled. "But you will be as soon as I can make my way to the bar. Another apple martini?"

"That would be nice."

"Stay right here. I'll return in a trice."

His hand disappeared from the small of her back and took some measure of confidence with it. She watched him walk into the large room to her right, skimming past women in Versace and Prada and men in Armani tuxedos, all of them perfectly coifed, smiling with even white teeth, holding drinks with their manicured hands.

Dash caused a remarkable stir. Everyone looked at him and either smiled broadly or moistened red lips, depending on the gender. Conversations broke midsentence. Men stepped back, stood up straighter. It unsettled her. She'd realized she'd be on display, but her imagination hadn't been up to the task. Being in the company of Dash Black had its price.

She didn't envy him this. How difficult to always be at the center. It was as if he'd run a gauntlet of starving beggars, and he was a juicy steak. Even from this distance, perhaps because of the distance, she could feel the pull on him. They all wanted something.

Was she any different? Sure, he'd asked her to this shindig, but still, hadn't she been doing the happy dance because she'd be with *him?* Didn't she fully expect the world to react to her differently?

Man, she needed a drink after that sobering thought. She inhaled deeply, trying to dispel some of her nervousness. As she let the breath go, she realized the focus of the crowd in the foyer had switched from Dash to her. Her first instinct was to hide. If she'd known where the bathroom was, she would have run. But Dash would be back soon, and then things would be all right.

The stares wouldn't quit. People were undoubtedly curious about who she was, but at least when Dash was next to her, he ran interference.

Maybe this wasn't such a great idea. Her jaw was starting to ache from holding her smile in place. Where was he?

A painting on the far wall caught her attention. She'd hardly registered her surroundings, which was astonishing considering the room. It was a foyer, and it was larger than her apartment. The floor was marble, the walls eggshell, and the décor screamed money.

The painting in question was a Monet, and she'd be willing to bet the house that it was real. No regular prints for the Nicklebys. Every piece, from the secretary under the mirror to the wall sconces were perfect and gorgeous. And so were the flower arrangements.

She headed over to the nearest pedestal, one of six that lined the room. Whoever did the flowers was a master. They were gorgeous and lush and perfectly suited that space. The central focus was calla lilies, her personal favorite, and the way the florist had used the stargazers was nothing short of exquisite.

"I should have known that's where you'd be."

She turned at Dash's voice. "They're fabulous."

"Certainly no more beautiful than the arrangements at the office."

"Flattery will get you everywhere."

"I'm counting on it."

She flushed a little at his rejoinder as he handed her the martini. He'd gotten himself a drink, too, more of what he'd had in the limo from the looks of it. "This house is amazing."

He looked around. "There is a certain art to ostentation, isn't there?"

"Indeed."

He took a sip of his drink and met her gaze. "Think you're ready for the ballroom?"

"Why not?"

He held out his arm. "Let's do it."

She linked her own arm with his, praying her trembling wouldn't spill her drink all over the floor. They

headed toward the sound of live music and the mur-
mur of a great many voices. She sipped her martini a
little too quickly, but dammit, she needed the courage.

The second they passed the doorway, she was
struck still at the size and scope of the party. The
music she'd heard was from an honest to God big
band, like Tommy Dorsey's or the Eddy Duchin Orchestra from the forties. They began "Moonlight Ser-
enade" as Dash guided her through the beautiful people.

The ballroom itself reminded her of the one from
Beauty and the Beast, including the domed ceiling.
Hundreds of sparkling lights dotted the dome and it
felt as though it was raining stars.

"Wow," she said.

"I know what you mean."

She caught the humor in his voice and sure enough,
when she looked at him he wore a gentle smile. "It
must be old hat for you."

He shrugged. "Being with you is remarkably re-
freshing. It's like seeing the place for the first time."

"I'm glad I can keep you entertained."

"Oh, there's no problem with that. In fact..." he
plucked her martini out of her hand and put it, along
with his drink, on the tray of a passing waiter.
"...come with me."

His arm went around her waist again, and nope, the
last time hadn't been a fluke. Her tummy did that
strange little dance and her breath caught as the heat
of him warmed her.

He led her to the dance floor, and the panic rose
again. She was about as good at dancing as she was
at bullfighting. The band was playing another Glen

Miller song, "String of Pearls," and the other couples on the dance floor swayed easily to the music. Maybe if you're rich enough, you could buy rhythm.

Dash grabbed her hand and swung her into his arms. They touched from chest to thighs, but by the time she opened her mouth to tell him she couldn't dance, they were.

His hand on the small of her back steered her with gentle caresses. Moving with incredible grace, he made it seem so easy. When she didn't step on his feet after the refrain, she relaxed. As much as she could, that is.

She smiled into his handsome face, and he rewarded her with a grin and a slight lift of his right brow. "You okay?"

"Yes," she said. "But don't get all excited and start doing a tango or anything."

"I promise. No tangos."

She thought of that film, *The American President*, when Annette Benning dances with Michael Douglas for the first time. When he tells her everyone in the room isn't looking at him, but at her.

If Tess didn't look around, she'd be okay. Of course it was no hardship to keep her gaze on Dash. The longer she stared at him, the more she liked his face. The more real he became.

They danced as if they'd danced a hundred times before, as if the music was made to order. He held her close enough for her to catch his spicy hint of cologne.

"So, what do you think, Ms. Norton? Is the ball to your liking?"

She thought a minute, wanting to get her answer

right. "It's a nice place to visit, but I'm not sure I'd want to live here."

He smiled. "No one really lives here. Even the Nicklebys are putting on the dog. It's a fantasy."

"Like our date?"

"On the contrary. It may have started out as a favor, but it's turning into my lucky night."

She shook her head. "I don't think you're going to be *that* lucky."

His laughter pleased her way too much. "Touché."

"I am grateful, though."

His smile faded. "You don't think I'm expecting anything in return, do you?"

"I don't know. I barely know you."

"Good point. Rest assured. I expect nothing."

She struggled to keep the disappointment from her face. "Thank you."

The song ended, but he didn't let her go. They stood, his hand still on her back, while couples shuffled around them. "Don't look now," he whispered, leaning in so only she could hear. "But there's Cullen."

She instantly tensed as she followed his gaze. Cullen stood by one of the bars, the one farthest from the band. He looked elegant and easy in his tuxedo. She'd met him only once before, and that was at a crowded restaurant. He'd seemed pleasant enough, but he hadn't been terribly interested in her. His willingness to look at her business plan was more of a favor to Brad than due to any excitement on his part.

He sipped some champagne as he canvassed the room. She watched him nod to a burly fellow, then again to a startlingly tall woman in a see-through blouse.

Tess figured he must be in his sixties. He had a thick mane of white hair with bushy matching brows. She wondered if he even remembered that they were supposed to meet here.

"Come on," Dash said.

"Wait."

"Okay."

She took a deep breath. "No. Let's go."

"Are you sure?"

She nodded. "No time like the present."

"You're going to knock his socks off."

"Oh, my God."

Dash led her slowly through the crowd. He could feel her tremble beneath his hand, but he doubted anyone could see her nervousness. She had handled this trip into the twilight zone with aplomb. He could see why she'd been so successful with her plant company.

Naturally, he'd done some checking on her. No need to be foolish, not in his position. Aside from the fact that Patrick liked her, the other recommendations he'd gotten had been glowing.

He didn't know Brad well, but the man was a fool. If it wasn't so impossible, he'd make a play for her himself. Not just for tonight, either. He'd like to get to know her, spend time with her. She was bright and witty and he liked the fact that she wasn't part of his crowd. Which was the problem. She didn't belong to his world. On a personal level, that meant nothing to him. Professionally, however, it was a different story.

Cullen was watching a busty blonde drink champagne, his gaze on her cleavage. Typical Cullen. The man had made some wise investments when a great many others had chosen poorly. His net worth was in the hundreds of millions. He did the venture capital bit because he enjoyed it. He liked to take risks on people, and he was rarely wrong. He was going to love Tess.

"Mr. Cullen?"

He looked up, slightly annoyed at being disturbed, but when he saw Tess he smiled. "Hello there."

"I'm not sure if you remember me. I'm Tess Norton. I met you a few weeks ago at Le Cirque."

His eyes narrowed. Dash knew he was drawing a blank.

"Jeez, Cullen, I hope you're investments are stronger than your memory."

"Dash Black, you scoundrel." Jim held out his hand, and Dash shook it firmly.

"I am a scoundrel indeed. But then, it takes one to know one."

Cullen laughed, then slid his gaze back to Tess.

"Tess was telling me that you're going to look at her business plan. I can see age hasn't dulled your good sense."

"So you're with Dash, eh?" Cullen asked Tess. "I should be worried about that. He's got something of a reputation."

"We're friends." Tess took a step away from him, and Dash sensed something wrong, although he couldn't imagine what.

"Friends?" Cullen's eyebrows rose with a hint of a leer. "He has good taste."

"Thank you. I just wanted to mention that you

should have my business plan at your office on Monday. I appreciate you taking the time to look at it.''

"It's all numbers," he said. "I don't invest to lose money."

"Of course not. I think you'll find I've put together a solid proposal."

He studied her more carefully. "I'll give you my honest appraisal, Ms. Norton. That's all I can promise."

She smiled, and Dash knew she had him. "That's all I ask."

"We'll be in touch."

Dash slapped Cullen on the back. "Good to see you, Jim. I'm sure you'll understand why I'm going to steal Tess away?"

"Lucky man."

"I am that, also."

Cullen laughed, then started searching for the breasts he'd found so appealing before their interruption.

Dash found Tess's hand and led her back toward the dance floor. Once they were well clear of Cullen, she pulled him to a stop.

"Mr. Black."

He frowned. "We're back to Mr. Black?"

"All right, Dash. I don't mean to sound ungrateful, but you didn't need to do that."

"Do what? Shake hands with an old friend?"

"I could have handled it myself."

"I know. You were doing great. My intention wasn't to interfere. Just to grease the wheels a bit."

She looked at him with puzzled eyes. "I should be thrilled. I am thrilled. It's just that…"

"You wanted to do this on your own."

"Yes."

"You did. You have. I'm just window dressing. If the man likes your proposal, it won't have a thing to do with me. That's not how Cullen works."

"I suppose you're right."

"I am. However, I apologize. I should have kept my big nose out of your affairs."

"No, no. That's not—I mean, I'm glad. I don't mind. Really. You were great."

Dash caught sight of a small woman with big diamonds. In addition to the sparklers on her wrist and neck, she also had possession of one Brad Sunderland. Lacey Talbot had arrived, and in style, too, from what he could see. Her entourage surrounded her like secret service agents. Lacey turned his way, and her eyes widened as she spied his date. A second later, Brad had a similar reaction.

Dash smiled as he looked into Tess's beautiful eyes. "Perhaps I can make it up to you," he whispered. Then he pulled her into his arms and kissed her like there was no tomorrow.

5

WHEN DASH'S MOUTH suddenly claimed hers she gasped roughly into the kiss; a hot, sinfully skillful tongue filled her and stroked the arched, sensitive vault of her mouth. The rawness, the heat, the unexpected invasion of wet and breath made Tess want to cry out with pleasure, but the sound of her desire came out as a strangled cry.

Oh, God—a rush of flame drove through every nerve in her body, down and farther down, until she was in danger of falling, weak and smoking, where she stood.

A flash of light behind her closed eyelids, and then it was over. She was back in the ballroom, standing beside him while the music still played, and laughter mixed with the clink of crystal sprinkled the air.

A man with a camera stood just behind Dash, and she made sense of the flash of light. She'd thought...well, that was silly. The reporter looked pleased, but Dash certainly didn't. In fact, Dash looked shocked as hell. Had he felt that...that whatever it was, too?

He pulled her into his arms again, holding her tight as he moved deeper into the crowd on the dance floor. The music was familiar, and if she took just a moment she'd figure out the piece, but then Dash leaned close, his warm breath on her ear making her shiver.

"Did you feel that?" he whispered.

"What?"

"The earth moved. The angels wept."

She smiled as heat filled her cheeks. "Oh, that."

He slowed his movements, and when he pressed up against her she could feel the heat of his erection. This time she didn't back away. At least, not so quickly. It felt wickedly wonderful to have such proof of his attraction to her. Her. Tess Norton, a nobody from nowhere.

The thought brought with it an awareness of how out of her element she was. An interloper with grand designs. The sudden switch in mood jarred her. She'd been so happy seconds ago. Dash turned her slowly, and when she caught sight of a perfectly coifed blonde, she understood more than just her reason for her unease. Lacey and Brad danced not ten feet away.

She watched them together until Brad turned in her direction. Averting her gaze, she lost her footing and stumbled, but Dash was there to catch her.

"Sorry."

"It's all right."

"And thank you."

He leaned back and looked at her questioningly. "For what?"

"The kiss. I just saw Brad and Lacey."

"Ah. They're a pair, aren't they? Such love and compassion for their fellow men. Always willing to lend a hand to the less fortunate."

"They are pretty snooty."

His brow arched. "Snooty? I suppose that's as good a description as any."

"Give me another drink, and I'll get much more vivid."

"I think I'd like to see you drunk."

"It's not pretty. I get very gregarious."

"Oh?"

"Not dancing on tabletops gregarious. Just real friendly."

"I like it more and more."

"Of course, I do have a tendency to fall asleep."

"Okay, scratch the bottle of scotch I was going to buy."

She grinned, but it didn't linger. Lacey came into view again, and this time, she was staring. Tess jerked her gaze back to Dash. "She hates me, you know."

"Hate? Isn't that pretty strong?"

Tess shook her head. "I don't think so. She's been quite ugly to me."

He moved her hand to his shoulder, then touched her cheek. "She's not a nice woman," he said, "and the best thing you could do is stay away from her."

"I try. But I still don't understand it. I never did anything to her."

"You didn't need to. You're attractive as hell and you're on her turf."

Tess squeezed his hand, but she didn't want to talk about this anymore. She was nervous enough without having to worry about Lacey. "You dance beautifully."

"Thank you. It's easy when my partner feels so good in my arms."

"You're even better at that."

"At what?"

"You know. No wonder the ladies all love you."

"I have no idea what you're talking about."

"Look, I'm flattered, but, you don't have to…"

"I don't have to what?"

"Seduce me."

"You think that's what I'm doing?"

Heat rushed to her cheeks. "Oh, God, I hope so."

He laughed out loud. "Can you blame me? God, Tess, you're a breath of fresh air."

She smiled, even if there was a twinge of something at the back of her mind. The music stopped and the moment passed. Dash led her toward the edge of the room where small tables had been set up. Waiters and waitresses passed around hors d'oeuvres, and it hit her that she was starving. She'd been so nervous all day, she'd barely had a bite.

Dash wrangled them a table, and then he went to replenish their drinks. She made them both plates of prawns, blini with caviar, lobster skewers, heavenly pot stickers, and endive leaves dotted with a spicy concoction she couldn't decipher. After she'd eaten one of everything, she looked around at her immediate neighbors. There were so many recognizable faces. The most famous were the Spielbergs, followed closely by David Letterman. Kim Bassinger sat in a far corner, and Tess thought she saw Neil Simon. And that was just the celebrity faction in the immediate vicinity. The editor of *Vogue* sat three seats away, and the president of Time/Warner held court near the bar. The net worth of the room was surely in the billions. Tess had eleven hundred dollars in the bank.

It didn't matter. She wasn't here to compete. Just

to meet up with Cullen, and that had gone well, so what was her problem? Not to mention Dash kissing her in front of Brad and Lacey, which was exactly what she'd hoped for. Odd how she'd been more upset by seeing Lacey. Brad had been fun, even if he tended to be inattentive at times. Not to mention his annoying little habit of canceling their plans without much notice. But, it didn't matter. Brad was right up there in her Men Not To Do List. Dash Black was at the top of the list, erection or no erection. Any thoughts of romance with him were plain out delusions. She wasn't going to go there.

At least not until he came back with their drinks. She sighed, and looked toward the bar, and Dash.

Dash excused himself from his chat with Ted Koppel the moment it felt right. He liked the man, found him interesting as hell, but Ted couldn't compete with the lady waiting for him.

It surprised him, this eagerness he felt. It had been a long while since he'd felt this sense of urgency. A spontaneous erection in the middle of a crowded room was an experience he'd thought he'd outgrown years ago. Christ, what was it about Tess? Sure, she was attractive, but that wasn't enough to get him this hot and bothered. Was it the freedom of being with a woman who expected nothing from him? That tonight he didn't have to do the dog and pony show? He had no idea. What did it matter? The night stretched ahead of him, filled with promise and if he was lucky…

Patrick's warning came back to him, and while he agreed that Tess wasn't to be treated in a cavalier fashion, he also saw no earthly reason they shouldn't indulge in some carnal pleasures. If the lady was so inclined, of course. Which she would be by the time the party ended. He'd make sure of it.

As he stood in line with about twenty other guests, studiously avoiding anyone's gaze, he caught a glimpse of something red on his sleeve. He looked more closely, still unable to identify it. He plucked the small plastic thing, not surprised that it was hard, but the shape—

Tess's fingernail. She must have lost it when they were dancing. He glanced her way, but his view was blocked. This could be a little tricky. He had to give it back to her, but when he did, she'd be embarrassed. Maybe there was a way to slip it back on her nail without her knowing. He'd never encountered this problem before. He'd have to give it some thought. But not at the moment. He'd finally made it to the head of the line. He slipped the nail in his pocket as he ordered their drinks.

It was difficult not to hurry the bartender along. Dash wanted to get back to her. He felt as if he'd been away for hours. That he was missing something exciting while the man searched for an open bottle of soda.

"Why, Dash Black. You little devil."

He knew the voice. Lacey Talbot. He pasted a smile on and turned to greet her. "Lacey."

She stood on tiptoe to give him a European kiss. No touching, just affectation. "How are you, Dash?"

"I'm just fine, Lacey, how about yourself?"

"Oh, you know me," she said, her gaze locked on his and ready to fire. "I make sure I'm always fine."

"Yes, I do know that about you. It's served you well."

She smiled, showing off her terrifically expensive bonding job. Not that he gave a damn about her teeth. Or any other part of her. He just wanted to take his drinks and go. But while he was with Tess, snubbing Lacey wasn't wise.

"I saw you with that little plant girl. What on earth?"

"She's my date, Lacey."

"Your date? And how did she arrange that?"

"I asked her."

"Come on, Dash, it's me. I know your type, and she isn't it. Except for perhaps a little slap and tickle on the limo ride home?"

"She's very much my type, and if you'll excuse me, she's waiting."

"Brad found her amusing, too. At least for a moment. Then he realized she was just another leech. Like all the other leeches."

"Speaking of Brad, he's looking for you. Last time I saw him, he was standing by a redhead in a white dress. I'll talk to you later."

"Watch yourself, Dash." All pretense of bonhomie had fled, and the basic Lacey was left. Vicious, petty, and not terribly attractive. "You could wind up with a nice little paternity suit if you're not careful."

One good thing about a life in the spotlight. In moments like these, he had a lot of practice holding his temper. "Thanks for the advice. Now, if you'll excuse me."

"Of course. Oh, there's Kate and Steven. Hello, Katy!"

He watched her move into position, insinuating herself out of sheer chutzpah. Damn little twit. If she was any smarter, she'd be dangerous. Unfortunately, she was an influential little twit. With enough money to buy and sell most third world countries, Lacey held a strange sort of power in the inner workings of New York's elite. It wasn't simply by dint of her checkbook, either. She was a necessary ingredient in a successful fund-raiser, and her blessings given to a social climber insured entrée into even the most coveted of soirées. But she was also something of a bitch, and she hated that she wasn't the most beautiful pearl on the necklace.

Dash grabbed his drinks and headed back toward the beautiful and infinitely more pleasant Tess. His step quickened as he reached their row of tables. Just watching her, unaware of his scrutiny, made him want her more. She looked interested, curious, and a little bit nervous. The women he dated tended to be "on" all the time. Even waiting at a table. Of course, he understood that. He had to be the same way. It was damn draining.

Tess didn't know what it was like to live in a fishbowl. To have every move scrutinized, every look interpreted through some salacious view finder. He envied her. The last thing she needed was to hang out with the likes of him. He was bad news for a girl like Tess.

Which didn't mean he didn't want to sleep with her.

"You're back."

"Sorry I was so long," he said, as he handed her her drink and sat down. "I got cornered."

"It's all right. Except I ate all your goodies."

He smiled. There, that was something new, different. Tess ate like a real person. He saw how his women friends suffered because of the unrealistic expectations of the media, and it bothered him. But as long as they wanted to continue to be movie stars or models, they had to settle for lettuce leaves and water with lemon.

He signaled a nearby waiter. "I'll get you some more."

"No, you'll get *you* some more. I'm fine."

"If that was dinner, you're not."

"I am. Honestly. I served us both pretty generously. I should have stopped with my own."

"I'm glad you didn't."

The waiter came by with stuffed oysters. Tess declined, and Dash took one, although he wasn't hungry. When they were alone again, he leaned closer, wishing they weren't in the middle of a crowded room. He wanted her alone. And not just because he wanted her naked. It was peculiar, actually. He hardly knew her, and yet... "You come from a small town, right?"

"Population two thousand, five hundred and counting."

"What made you decide to come to New York?"

"Population two thousand, five hundred and counting."

He grinned. "I see. And now that you're here?"

She swept a hair off her temple, and his gaze followed the movement. Her skin was so soft, he wanted to touch her again. "It's bigger," she said. "But it's wonderful. Even after nine-eleven, It's still the best city in the world. Hey, maybe because of nine-eleven,

I don't know. I'm just glad I'm here, and I hope to stay for a long time.''

"This flower shop. Have you always wanted one?''

"No. When I lived in Texas I wasn't sure what I wanted to do. Except escape. I got hooked up with the plant thing by accident. I loved it. Felt instantly at home. I took a bunch of classes at the junior college, and voilà. Here I am.''

"Voilà, huh? I have a feeling you told me the Disney version.''

"Not really. As far as my career has gone, New York has been good to me.''

"And your personal life?''

"Whole other ball game.''

"Want to talk about it?''

She shook her head. "I don't think so. I don't know you well enough to share my tragic love life.''

"I already know about Brad.''

"That wasn't tragic. Pathetic, maybe, but not tragic.''

"Did someone hurt you?''

She studied her glass, and Dash noticed the finger that was missing a nail. Not the right time to mention it. He'd wait. When she didn't respond, he almost changed the subject. Instead, he touched her arm. "Would you like to go outside?''

Her gaze swung up to meet his. "Yes, I would.''

He stood up and extended his hand.

Tess felt like royalty as he helped her to her feet. Just being next to him made her giddy, but when he proceeded to put his arm around her waist, it was almost too much.

She still hadn't figured it out. Was this incredible

pull only there because he was the infamous Dash Black? Or was it the basic man who drew her like a spoon to a magnet. How was it possible to separate the man from the celebrity? The only time she felt totally at ease with him was when they talked. Once in conversation, she could focus.

Walking across the room was a whole different matter. It felt as if every eye was upon them, and it wasn't just paranoia speaking. Every time she let her glance stray to one side or the other, she met covetous stares. Men, women, young, old, it didn't matter. They wanted him. They wanted to be near him in case his magic somehow rubbed off. She couldn't blame them. She wanted it, too.

One small benefit of his celebrity was that people did tend to get out of his way. They were at the patio doors halfway through the opening stanza of "My Funny Valentine."

The cool air felt delicious as it washed over her. Dash led her down the steps to a stone path that meandered past Carolina hemlock trees and small bushes of jasmine that filled the night with perfume. She wondered if the perfect night had been purchased by the Nicklebys, if even the gods wouldn't dare mar their party with rain or cold. The music from the ballroom wafted gently among the leaves, and if there was a more perfect moment in her life, Tess couldn't remember it.

She wanted everything to stop right here. And if it couldn't, she wanted her memory to be very, very good.

Dash squeezed her waist, bringing her closer to him. As astonishing as it was, she knew he wanted her. What she didn't know was if it was because she was a novelty, because he felt compelled to sleep with every woman in reach, or if he liked her. What she also didn't know was if she cared.

This was Dash Black. The one, the only. He was everything dreams are made of and he wanted her. At least for tonight. Which made him the personification of the man she'd sworn to avoid. Or did it? She couldn't really group him with anyone else. He was outside the loop, apart from all those mere mortals.

He brought her to a pond, a dark smooth surface hidden by lush vegetation studded with tiny white lights. It was something out of a fairy tale.

He must have been there before to have found it. While they'd passed one or two couples on the path, no one was nearby now.

The hand at her waist moved slowly up her back. Using some strange alchemy, he moved in front of her without her knowing how. His gaze found hers and held her steady. He leaned slowly forward until she felt his warm breath.

Then he kissed her.

Slowly, softly, with a gentleness that made her knees weak. His tongue touched the inside of her lips, and she breathed him in, met his caress with one of her own.

He pulled her closer, so they were chest to chest, hips to hips, and her arms curled around his neck.

He moaned, and she drifted in a state of pure bliss as he thoroughly, patiently, sweetly explored every inch of her mouth. It wasn't just a kiss, in the same way Dash wasn't just a man. His taste stole her breath, his scent stole her senses, and his body stole her will.

She could hardly believe it when he pulled back, when he met her gaze again, and let her go. Her hurt must have shown because he frowned in sympathy.

"I think you're very brave, Tess Norton. I admire the way you're going after your future. How you've seized the day. You deserve all the success and happiness in the world, and I'm glad I could help in my own little way."

"But?" she asked, not sure she wanted to hear the rest.

"You need me like a hole in the head. You're as enticing a woman as I've ever seen, so don't you dare think otherwise. But this isn't supposed to be. If I wasn't such a selfish bastard, I'd have kept my hands to myself all night. You were too tempting."

"And now I'm chopped liver?"

He laughed, filling the air with his deep baritone. "No. You're a special woman, Tess. When I say you don't need me to mess things up, you'd better believe it."

"What if I want things messy?"

He leaned forward until his warm breath fanned her cheek. "Be careful what you wish for."

Dash's whisper slid into her ear and uncoiled there like a kiss, tempting and serpentine. "Because I might get it?"

He nodded. Touched her cheek with the back of his hand. And she sighed as he kissed her once more.

6

TESS TRIED TO TELL herself that she was too ordinary for a man like Dash. She tried to tell herself that she would pay for this dip into sin in ways countless and unforeseeable, that she was doing the exact thing she'd sworn was the worst thing she could do…but she wasn't listening to herself. She didn't care.

A warm, laugh-laden breath burst gently into Tess's own open mouth, followed immediately by a soft groan that sent tickling reverberations down her throat, and lower. He brought her closer, filling her with remarkable sensations from head to toe, a range that contained the scratch of barely there whiskers, fine cloth against bare skin, and flexing muscle. The moon, indecisive, had retreated again, but the splash of lights from the trees remained and bathed them in a luminous glow that seemed the very aura of their desire.

Breaking the kiss, Tess rubbed her cheek against Dash's jaw and neck, and then against the hard curve of his shoulder. Arms tightened around her, hands seized and searched the flesh of her back as if to give comfort. But it wasn't comfort that was being offered. The intoxicating scent of Dash's body—a hint of spice and soap—slipped through her common sense and reason. Yet she knew what she was getting into, and that it was likely to be very untidy, quite complicated. On the other hand, it could turn out to be her one perfect night.

"Tess, you're a dangerous woman."

"Yeah, that's me all over."

"I'm not kidding. I'm not sure I can let you go."

"And that's scary...how?"

He chuckled, and she felt the vibrations in her chest. "I'm not in a position to make this more than tonight."

She'd known it, but hearing him made her sigh. "Great, I find the one honest man in Long Island."

His finger touched her chin and lifted her gaze to his. "I'm not saying it to be mean. I don't want you to get hurt."

"I hate to disillusion you, Dash, but I'm not a blushing virgin. I've had the occasional one-night stand."

"Did you enjoy them?"

She shifted away from his touch. "At the time? Yes."

"And the next day?"

"We're not talking about double digits or anything here. In fact, you can count my wild nights on one hand."

"You didn't answer me."

"There was one night, yes, that was incredible. I have no regrets about that one at all."

"What made it so special?"

Her cheeks heated. "Are we really going to talk about my night with another man?"

"Not in specifics, I hope," he said. "But I am curious."

"He was honest, like you. And he was leaving the next day for a job in Milan."

"Hell of a way to say bon voyage."

She nodded, not wanting to talk about Lawrence anymore. She'd told Dash the truth. It had been a perfect night, and she'd never been sorry.

"I'm not leaving for Milan," Dash said. "I'm still going to live in the same apartment. Work in the same office."

"And you don't need a lovesick plant lady moping around, is that it?"

He touched her arm. "I don't want either of us getting into something we shouldn't."

She hugged her own waist, knowing he was right. That she had no business kissing this man, let alone ripping off his clothes, throwing him on the nearest available surface and milking him dry. Not that she'd been thinking about it or anything, but jeez. What was she going to tell her grandchildren? *"Sorry, kids, but granny couldn't pull it off. It ended with a kiss."*

"Are you cold?"

"No. Just ready to go back inside."

"For what it's worth, I'm damn disappointed."

"Don't be. I'm not that good in the sack."

He laughed again. "I seriously doubt that."

"No, it's true. I'm pushy and demanding and I go right to sleep afterward. You're much better off."

He groaned. "You've just described my ideal woman."

"You say that now, but when I'm sawing logs and you want to cuddle, you'll be calling me all sorts of unattractive names."

His arm went around her shoulders. "Maybe I've been hasty here."

"Maybe you've been smart. God knows, one of us needed to be."

"Still…"

"I hear music. Cole Porter, I believe."

"Point taken."

They walked back up the path while Tess tried not to be too bummed out. She wished she could at least talk to Sam and Erin. They would be wise and knowing, and with her happiness firmly in mind, convince her to shut up and attack the guy.

"If you'd like, I'll take you around and introduce you to some people I think you might find interesting."

"That would be wonderful."

"And I'm going to depend on you to say when we go home."

"Isn't there a minimum stay required?"

"Only for the valets."

"Okay. I promise not to keep you up too late."

"Don't worry about me. As long as you're here, I'm having a good time."

"Oh, yeah? Wait till they start charades. I kick butt at charades, and I'm afraid I'd just make you look bad."

"Hmm, I'm trying to remember the last time I played charades with the Nicklebys. That would be…never."

"What? All this room, all these people and no parlor games? What kind of rip-off is this?"

He laughed. Such a good sound. "Next time, let's

go to one of your friend's parties. I think we'd both have more fun."

"But then, the Spielbergs so rarely drop by Mary's."

"Their loss."

They reached the patio, which had gotten quite crowded. Mostly, she imagined, those who had worked up a sweat on the dance floor. No sign of Lacey or Brad, which was a good thing.

They stopped twice on their way inside when Dash introduced her to Chris Noth and Peter Frechette, both high up on her list of favorite actors. Dash included her so smoothly into the conversations, anyone would think she belonged there.

When they were alone again, she begged off to the rest room, a huge affair with stalls, á la fine hotels, two attendants and more beauty supply accoutrements than her local drug store. It was a bit disconcerting to know the woman in the stall next to her was Uma Thurman. Although, she had to suppress a giggle as she realized once and for all that yes, famous movie stars go to the bathroom just like everyone else.

Tess availed herself of some hand cream, a few swipes of mascara (packaged for one use only) and a toothbrush (ditto). After a final fluff of hair, she reentered the fray, searching the crowd for Dash.

She didn't spot him. She did spot Lacey. Talking to Cullen. Cullen didn't look pleased.

Tess tensed immediately, and even as the dialogue in her head assured her that of course they knew each other, and that they had no reason on earth to be talking about *her,* she somehow felt certain they were.

She edged toward them, but there wasn't a way to

hear the conversation without showing herself. Where the hell was Dash? He could run interference. Step in. Sway the conversation. The hell with doing it on her own. If she'd had a red flare, she'd have set it off.

The best way to find Dash, she decided, was by looking for a gaggle of females. Dash was sure to be in the middle. She scanned the area near the closest bar with no luck, then she hit pay dirt. Sure enough, several gorgeous females had Dash surrounded.

Tess hurried over, walking carefully in back of Lacey and Cullen. By the time she reached Dash's party, she was in a state.

Bless his heart, he saw it right away. He excused himself from his admiring throng and poised at her side. "What's wrong?"

She turned toward the twosome still deep in discussion. "Look who found Cullen."

Dash followed her gaze. Cullen had lowered his head to bring it closer to Lacey's ear. Lacey seemed a woman with a mission, and Dash understood immediately why Tess was upset. "They've known each other for a long time," he said.

"So I've told myself."

"It's not necessarily about you."

"Uh-huh."

"Do you want me to go over there?"

She looked up at him with her big dark eyes wide and hopeful. "Would you mind?"

"Not at all. You stay here. I'd get you a drink, but I think you need to keep busy. I'll be back at oh-five-hundred."

He got a smile out of her, which was good. Lacey bending Cullen's ear couldn't be good. Dash headed toward them, quite prepared to defend his lady's honor.

His suspicions were confirmed the second Lacey spotted him. She stopped talking, midsentence, and her cheeks grew uncharacteristically pink.

"Hello, Lacey. Funny meeting you here."

"Hello, Dash."

He nodded at the older man. "I didn't know you two were so close."

Cullen didn't look at him. "Close enough."

"So what were we talking about?"

Cullen's expression told him everything. So did Lacey's smug smile. "Bored, are we, Lacey?"

"Far from it."

"Come on. You've been talking about Tess, haven't you?"

"What if we have?"

"She's with me tonight. And I'm not real fond of having my date talked about behind her back."

"If she wants to come over here, I'll say it to her face."

"Say what?"

"That she's a climber. That she has no background, no breeding. That she's already been with half the men on the West side. I'm not surprised she ended up here with you. You're a soft touch, Dash."

"And how did you get to be such an expert on her?"

"I pay attention. It's all common knowledge, Dash. If you know who to listen to."

What would it feel like to have to be that petty? Dash shook his head. Lacey wasn't bad looking. It was her black heart that made her so unattractive.

Since he couldn't strangle her with his bare hands, he decided on the next best thing. He'd ignore her completely.

He turned to Cullen, stepping closer to the older man. "Jim, we've known each other for a long time. I'm telling you to take a strong look at this girl's proposal. I think she's a good bet."

"Then why aren't you financing her?" Lacey asked.

He continued to ignore the woman. "I'll give you a call, Jim. On Monday."

For the first time since he'd approached, Cullen looked Dash square in the eyes. It wasn't warm and fuzzy. "I'll talk to you, Dash, but I'll be doing some checking of my own. I'll make my own decision."

"Fair enough. Now, if you'll excuse me, a lovely lady awaits." He nodded at Cullen, and left without another glance at Lacey.

What he needed to do was calm down before he met up with Tess. She was a sharp girl, and she'd realize things hadn't gone well. Actually, the news wasn't bad. Dash had expected Cullen to do his homework regardless of Lacey's gossip. And he was sure it was just that.

Admittedly, he didn't know Tess well, but if Patrick had hired her, then she had to be on the up and up. Patrick was rarely fooled, and he was fiercely protective of anything to do with Noir. So Cullen would do his search, and he'd see that Tess would be a good risk.

Dash smiled as he caught sight of her, and the business with Lacey shifted to the blurry past. Tess hadn't seen him yet. He could tell she was anxious, mostly by the set of her shoulders, but a stranger wouldn't. She was poised, lovely, confident. And that red dress...Jesus, but that was some dress.

A man Dash didn't know evidently had the same response. He stared unabashedly at her, a lascivious gleam in his eye. He was a pretty good-looking bastard. Dash hurried.

"Tell me everything's okay," she said, the moment he was at her side. "Please. I've imagined every horrible thing."

"It's all right."

"You're just saying that."

He laughed at her logic. "No, I'm not. Everything's going to be fine. Cullen is going to judge you on your merits, not anything Lacey could say."

"So she was talking about me."

Shit. He didn't know what to do here. Lie and make Tess feel better? Or tell the truth, but reassure her? He had the feeling she'd want him to be straight. "Yes, she was. But don't get upset. Cullen isn't the man he is today because he listened to gossip. He's going to research you and your proposal for himself. So there's nothing to worry about."

She stared at him, but he doubted she saw him. He imagined she was reviewing her life, probably from birth on, to see if she'd pass muster.

"Tess?"

It took her a few seconds to focus. "Yes?"

"Have you ever killed anyone?"

Her brows furrowed as she frowned. "No."

"Robbed any banks? Been convicted of a felony?"

"Of course not."

"No major crimes or huge skeletons in your closet?"

"My uncle once stole a barbecue recipe from the state cook-off champions, which caused a serious uproar in five counties. That would be the extent of my criminal involvement."

"Great. So, as I said, there's nothing to worry about."

"Except what Lacey told him."

"Lacey isn't going to sway him."

"Lacey seems to sway everything around here."

"Have faith." He put his arm around her and pulled her close. "I believe in you. And I'm not a pushover."

"No, you're just horny."

He grinned. "That's true. But that doesn't discount the other."

"It doesn't help."

"Tess, you're too young to be so cynical."

"It's not cynicism. It's the truth. You know, you men can be quite silly."

"Oh?"

She nodded. He rubbed her back, enjoying the feel of her skin beneath his hand. They weren't dancing, but they were swaying to the music. The band played one of his favorite pieces, the theme from *Laura*, the old movie with Dana Andrews and Jean Tierney. Now, that was romance.

"Yes, silly. I'll just give you one example. Fist-fights."

"I'm not arguing. But go on. Tell me your theory on fistfights."

"I had one, you know. When I was in fifth grade.

I had this friend. Well, not really a friend. An arch enemy would be closer to the truth.''

"Arch enemy? Like Lex Luthor?''

"Yeah, but she had more hair. Anyway, she and I got into it one day, and we squared off in the playground. I hit her, which wasn't so bad, although it was a little unsettling. But then she hit me. It hurt like a mother!''

He leaned back to look at her. "What did you expect?''

"Not that. I saw fights on TV all the time. No one even said ouch. I mean, I was expecting great sound effects, fast-paced music, a commercial break. Not pain.''

"So what did you do?''

"I stopped fighting. Right then. We both did. And I've never been in a fistfight since.''

"And men?''

"They get into them all the time. It's crazy.''

"I suppose I can go along with that. Men are crazy when it comes to fistfights.''

"Okay, then. And there are lots of other things, too.''

"I'd like to hear all of them.''

"That would take too much time.''

He ran the back of his finger down her cheek. "And yet you still date them. These silly men.''

She sighed. "I know I can't help it. I like them.''

"I believe I speak for all of my gender when I say we're glad you do.''

Her smile stirred him again. A gentle nudge that made him want to get uninhibitedly silly under the nearest table. And fistfighting would not be involved.

"Thank you," she whispered.

"For what?"

"For talking to Cullen. I know I asked you to stay out of it, then did a complete one-eighty. I appreciate it."

"Doing it on your own doesn't mean you can't ask for help."

She nodded. "I'm just so stunned about Lacey... I can't figure her out."

"Women can be very silly, too."

She grinned. "Yes, they can."

"Do you want to dance some more?"

She shook her head. "I think I'd like some champagne. And a quiet spot to sit while we drink it."

He bowed. "I'm at your service, mademoiselle. It will only take a moment to get the bottle, and I have just the place in mind."

"I like going to parties with you," she said.

He leaned over and brushed his lips against hers. "I'm glad. Now, stay put. I'll be right back."

"They couldn't drag me away." Tess watched him make his way to the bar. She was in serious trouble here. Oh, yeah.

7

TESS DIDN'T MOVE FROM HER place between the bar and the patio door. She didn't want to risk bumping into Lacey. Or Brad. But especially Lacey.

Despite Dash's assurance that all was well, Tess had a very bad feeling. If Cullen passed, she'd have to do some quick footwork. New York was so incredibly expensive that she'd had to concentrate all her resources and energy into her business. She'd made it this long by scrimping and saving like a demon. Top Ramen, mac and cheese, day-old bread. She tried to be very subtle about it. When she was in the company of others, she didn't buy much, but she didn't claim poverty, either.

It was worth every skipped steak. Her dream was finally within reach. Unless Ms. Bitch had screwed it up for her.

She caught a glimpse of Dash, champagne bottle and two glasses in hand. He had a small cadre of women around him, and there wasn't much room for him to maneuver away. One of the women was an actress from one of Mary's soap operas. Tess couldn't think of her name. She was movie-star stunning, though, with long auburn hair and lips the size of waffle irons. Her breasts seemed to be aggressively seeking freedom from the confines of her dress and the woman clearly thought Dash should be *thisclose* when her boobs made it over the fence, so to speak.

Dash looked over at Tess and gave her an arched brow to let her know she wasn't forgotten. A few seconds later, the women laughed, and he, instead of the bountiful bosom, escaped.

The sick feeling she had about Lacey diminished as Dash got closer. There were only so many intense emotions one could feel at a time, and Dash demanded his due. He made it so easy to like him. He listened, he laughed on cue, he never let his focus wander. A dream date, in every respect. Except for the fact there was absolutely no future with him.

"Ready?" he said as he sidled in next to her.

"Very."

"Keep close. This may require some evasive action."

"I'm right with you, Captain."

"Captain? As in, 'Oh, Captain, My Captain?'"

"Somehow I can't picture you as Abe Lincoln. I was thinking more of Ahab."

"Peg leg and all?"

"No, just a large harpoon."

He stopped so suddenly she bumped into him, and then he laughed. Laughed loudly enough to cause quite a stir. She, on the other hand, blushed like a fool. She couldn't believe she'd just said that. Oh, God, her mouth would be the death of her yet.

He turned, still chuckling and kissed her on the tip of her nose. "I like going to parties with you, too."

She couldn't think of one witty thing to say about that. So she just smiled. He continued on, weaving through dancing, chatting, mingling, staring clusters of party attendees, some of them so famous that if she'd seen them under other circumstances, she'd have gawked like a ten-year-old. Tonight they held surprisingly little allure. She was already with the best of them. Maybe not the most famous, but certainly the handsomest. The most charming. The best dancer. She forced herself to stop there. No need to torture herself further. She was Cinderella without the glass slipper. All she'd ever have was this one ball. So she'd better milk it dry.

He hit the patio and waited for her to be at his side. Then he nodded to his right, and they found a new set of stairs leading to another path.

"It's this way," he said.

"What is?"

"Privacy," he said.

"Ah."

They walked past more gorgeous manicured greenery, softly lit by recessed lights in the ground. The music dimmed as they circled a greenhouse. The estate was so huge it simply boggled the mind. Who could actually live here? Besides the entire population of Rhode Island, of course. It was just so…impersonal. She would surely get tired of it in a year or two.

"What are you chuckling about?"

She hadn't realized it had been out loud. "This place is amazing. It doesn't feel like real life."

"It's not. It's bizarre in the extreme. More like a small country than a home."

"So you don't have one of these socked away in Southampton or Montauk?"

"No. But I do have a place in Park City. I like to ski."

"Fair enough."

"Now, my father has a place in Cannes, another in Palm Springs, a penthouse in Vegas and a yacht currently moored in Greece."

"No kidding. Me, too!"

He smiled, and hooked his arm around her waist, the champagne bottle bumping her hip. "It's pretty obscene."

"I don't know. Noir is famous for its charity work and community involvement. That makes a big difference."

"True."

"I've always wanted to go to the big gala. It looks so glamorous."

"Done. I'll make sure you get an invitation, and a VIP pass."

"I didn't mean—"

"I know. But I derive great pleasure from the rare moments I can give a woman exactly what she wants."

"Rare? I doubt that."

"Don't. It's true. Usually, the women I'm with want one of two things. A shill, so they don't have to date some untamed costar who can't keep his hands to himself, or they want the Dash Black they see in the papers."

"And you're not either of those things?"

"The first, absolutely. I offer a safe haven for anguished starlets. The second, not in the least."

"Now that I've had a small taste, I would beg to differ."

"Hold that thought." He let her go, walked up ahead, looking to the right then the left. He nodded left. "There it is."

She hurried to reach him and follow his gaze. There was a large building, about the size of a normal house. Behind it were several bungalows. Ivy nearly covered the outside of all the structures, and Tess felt a little creeped out. "What is that?" she whispered.

"I'll show you," he whispered back. Then he laughed, but it was a phony "bwahahaha" of a television bad guy.

"I don't know. Maybe I'd better get back to the party."

Dash's evil grin fell instantly as he blinked up at her. "Okay. Let's go."

She slugged him in the arm. "Ha ha."

"Whatever I can do to make your evening a superior experience..."

"You're certifiable, aren't you? You just don't show it in public."

"I have ways of making you keep my secret."

"I'll bet you do."

He bumped her with his shoulder. "Come on, woman. Let's get inside before I shake this champagne to death."

She followed him, her heart rate accelerating, anticipation making her breathe fast and hard. As they got closer to the big building she guessed it might be another greenhouse. But it was so huge. A guest house? Maybe.

It turned out to be a swimming pool.

As soon as they walked inside, lights came on, although they were so diffuse they were only intended to prevent people from falling in the water, not to read by. She was more drawn by the lights inside the Olympic-size pool. Absolutely still, the water was the perfect magnifier for the amazing design painted over the whole bottom surface. A mermaid. Beautiful, blond hair swirling, her full breasts exposed, her tail shimmering with rainbow-tinted scales. The artist had created magic.

"What do you think?" he asked.

"Ah, heck. You've seen one indoor swimming pool mermaid, you've seen them all."

"So cynical for one so pretty."

"I know. I'm a tough cookie. I don't get dazzled very easily."

"Uh-huh."

She swung around to look at him. "You don't believe me, do you?"

"Nope."

"Smart man."

"If I was truly smart, this champagne would already be open and we'd be toasting each other by now."

"Don't put it off on my account."

He went over to a table on the side of the pool and while he did champagne duty, she looked around the warm room. Aside from the pool itself, there was a long bar, something you'd expect to see at a resort. Spigots, glasses, bottles and bottles of every kind of spirit were all on display, and as she got closer she saw dispensers for sodas, ice cream, syrup. A full service bar for the whole family. Must be nice.

She passed another set of tables and chairs on her way to the doors at the far side of the room. There she found a bathroom, perfectly appointed and about as big as her apartment. Next to that was a changing room with separate stalls, and finally a room for miscellaneous furniture, pool toys and cleaning supplies.

The pop of the cork urged her back toward Dash. She walked slowly, wondering just what he had in mind. When he'd said private, he meant private. He probably wanted more than a glass of champagne, although she had no doubt whatsoever that he wouldn't push her into anything, except maybe the pool.

He'd poured the bubbly into both glasses, and held hers out to her. She took it, their fingers touching on the crystal. A frisson skittered down her back, and she wondered if he had seen her reaction in the dim light.

"To a beautiful woman," he said, his voice echoing slightly off the walls.

"To my hero," she replied, knowing she was a sip or two away from a decision. It would have been better if she had a clue what to do.

He sipped. She sipped. The slightly humid, warm air caressed her bare skin. There was just enough light for her to see the question in his gaze.

With a word, she could shift the tide in either direction. She wasn't usually indecisive. Not about sex. She had a healthy, normal drive and she saw nothing wrong with being intimate if the right opportunity arose. She wasn't promiscuous; far from it. The men in her life had all been special in some way.

Dash was special in a lot of ways.

Oh, this was going to drive her crazy. She didn't

believe in regrets. If she did this, she'd do it with her whole heart. And if she didn't?

That was the rub. The heat between them was undeniable. The attraction mutual. The atmosphere perfect. So what was she waiting for? How many times had she said to her friends that she'd sleep with Dash Black in a heartbeat? Of course, that was before she even dreamed she'd meet the man let alone be in a position to make it come true.

Dash Black. The sexiest man on earth. And hers for the asking.

"What's wrong?"

"What do you mean?"

He stepped closer. "You moaned."

"I did?"

"And you don't look very happy. Are you feeling all right?"

The concern on his face was genuine, of that she was sure. He'd never say a word to her if she chose to make things friendly but platonic. Which is what made up her mind. "I'm fine now," she said as she put her glass down on the table.

She took that one step. The one that would change the night, change everything. Dammit, why shouldn't she? He was incredible. And she was young, single and all alone with him.

She brushed his arm with her fingertips. He inhaled sharply, then put his glass next to hers.

"Tess," he whispered as his hand pulled her close. His lips brushed hers lightly, rubbed back and forth with such gentle teasing. Her eyes fluttered closed as she inhaled his champagne breath, as she relaxed her body, leaning against him, letting his strength carry her.

His hand skimmed over her back, over the bare skin above her dress, almost tickling, sensitizing, making her fight not to move.

A touch of his tongue on her lower lip, a sigh, his other hand stroked her arm as if she were a pampered cat. She held on to him, rocked ever so slightly back and forth as she tasted him, then withdrew.

"Tess," he murmured her name so she could taste it, then the kiss deepened.

The sultry air, the echo of their breathing, the shivery tingles from his teasing touch... Aware of each, aware of nothing but the promise of the next second.

"What do you like, Tess?" he asked softly, caressing her with the light, padded curve of his thumb, bringing it back down along the arch of her cheek, then running it along her lips. "What do you want me to do to you?"

"*To* me?" she asked with interest, eyelids lowering another notch.

"To you, with you...for you."

"Everything," she said, leaning forward to swipe another taste of his lips.

"That sounds perfect." He traced, with kisses, the line his thumb had made.

"I thought so."

"Only..."

"What?" she asked as her hand curved around the nape of his neck.

"Are you sure?"

She nodded.

"Good."

She nodded again. "Very good."

"No," he said as his lips lowered to hers. "*This* is very good."

She melted. Flowed into a puddle of mush as he showed her again why he was the sexiest man on the planet. He stroked, sucked, darted, lingered in a way that brought the simple kiss into the realm of high art. She'd never felt anything like it, and she'd kissed a few boys in her time. They all should be ashamed.

He did something seriously hot with the tip of his tongue, and her fingers corded through his hair to make absolutely, positively certain he wasn't going anywhere.

As his hand slid down the curve of her ass, she pressed against him tighter. If this was how he kissed, my God, how would he make love? How would she survive finding out?

The hand on her behind was confident, so was the erection pressing against her hip. He moved just enough to start the friction, to get her motor purring. And then he pulled away, leaving her openmouthed and disappointed.

His smile told her he wasn't finished…that he hadn't really started. His gaze told her he was going to make sure she never forgot this night.

He slipped off his tuxedo jacket, then undid his tie. She didn't move a muscle, just watched as he continued to undress. It wasn't a striptease or anything. There were no bumps, no grinds. But it was incredibly sexy to watch this man reveal himself to her piece by piece.

When the shirt came off, she had to steady herself against the bar behind her. His chest. Holy mother of…it was the chest that all other chests in the male kingdom would be measured against. Perfectly muscled, just enough golden tan, ditto with the light dusting of dark hair, it made her want to lick him from shoulder to shoulder and then straight on down till she hit pay dirt or died of sheer pleasure.

Pictures didn't do him justice. Hell, Michelangelo couldn't do him justice.

Then his hand went to his belt. She whimpered. Held tight to the bar so if her legs gave out, she wouldn't fall and break something. He pulled the leather tongue out of the loop, leaving his button exposed. A moment later that was undone, and his fingers were on his zipper.

She stopped breathing. Stopped any movement except for her thudding heart. The sound of the zipper lowering echoed off the walls and stirred her up like a milkshake.

But that was nothing compared to his next move. Leaving his fly open, with just a hint of black silk visible, he brought his hand slowly up his stomach, his abs, his chest, leading her gaze inexorably higher until his fingers were level with his nipples.

He swerved right, and touched himself there, making himself hard with a flick of his thumb. She'd never wanted to suck a nipple so badly in her life. She'd never given men's nipples much thought, and now she could see the error of her ways. Quarter-sized areolas begged to be licked, tasted. Followed by a full-out banquet on his hard little nubs.

She inhaled sharply, dizzy from holding her breath so long. With tremendous effort, she shifted her gaze to his face, to his wicked grin.

He caught her off guard with a wink, which, oddly enough, did very strange things to her insides and caused her to press her legs tightly together. Then his hands went to his trousers, and he lowered them inch by slow inch.

It took her a minute to realize his underwear was going right along with the pants, but once she did figure it out, she froze. Her gaze didn't waver, she didn't even blink. She just watched as more flesh came into view.

A dark line of hair pointed to the promised land, and then she saw the head of his cock, and oh, sweet jesus, he was thick and hard and long enough to rock her world until next week.

She breathed again, a gasp that bounced against the walls, as his pants slipped down and he stepped out of them. He stood before her, in this odd, warm room with the mermaid and the soft lights, naked and so stunning it almost hurt to look at him.

"One of us," he whispered, taking a step toward her, "is quite overdressed."

Her hand went to her stomach, surprised that she was, indeed still wearing her dress, her shoes. Hell, it shocked her that she was still upright.

He approached her slowly, allowing her to look at everything, especially the way the head of his cock tapped his taut stomach.

She sighed as he stepped behind her, but used the break to come back down to earth. This was unbelievable. He was more gorgeous than anyone she'd ever seen, man or woman, and oh, no, he was unzipping her dress, and it was gonna fall, and she was *way* outclassed here.

With one hand, she caught her dress, holding it tight. She couldn't do it. Not after seeing him. He was caviar and she was…cottage cheese.

He kissed the curve of her shoulder, then ran his hand down her arm. And somehow, when he touched her, she stopped being afraid. As his fingers skimmed the back of her hand, she let go.

8

DASH'S GAZE FOLLOWED THE path her dress had taken, although his journey took a lot longer. He couldn't seem to get past her breasts. They were incredible. Lush, round, pale, with long nipples, nipples that begged to be tasted. Each time she took a breath it was a religious experience. Someone should write a symphony to those hard little pearls.

Wresting his gaze from that perfection, he wandered down her body, appreciating more than words her curves, her womanliness. She reminded him of a violin. The small waist leading to lush hips, she was a masterpiece of femininity. A Stradivarius.

When he thought he could handle it, he looked down a bit farther. Her only undergarment was a pair of white panties. They were actually rather ordinary, not thongs or anything exotic. They hugged her close, rode high on her hips, let him see her belly button. He'd never seen a sight quite so erotic.

"Dash?"

He looked up into large, dark eyes, and he had to move close to her. Touch her. He lifted her hair and nuzzled the soft skin at the curve of her neck. "Hmm?"

"Hmm, what?"

"You said Dash."

"I did?"

He nodded.

Tess moaned and rubbed her chest against his. "It must not have been important."

"No doubt," he mumbled, as his right hand glided down her back until he found the waistband of her innocent panties.

"Dash?"

"Hmm?"

She turned her head, offering him her lips, slightly parted. Who was he to refuse? He kissed her softly as his fingers slipped down over her delectable ass.

Tess squirmed in his arms rubbing his chest and his cock, making it necessary and prudent to remove his hand from down under, take a few steps back and get a grip.

"Dash?"

"Hmm?"

"Why did you stop?"

"I didn't stop."

She frowned prettily. "You're over there."

"Only a step away."

"That's too far."

"It won't be for long. But I want you to do something for me, Tess."

"What's that?"

"I want you to take off your panties."

She looked down at herself, as if surprised she had anything on. In a flash, her thumbs hooked the waistband and lowered the garment past her hips. They dropped on her shoes, and in a one-two step, she was clear, the panties were on the puddle that was her dress, and she was gloriously naked.

He couldn't help but laugh. She had a way about her... He nodded, gestured her to come closer. Tess didn't make this move as quickly. She walked slowly and deliberately, exaggerating the sway of her hips. Her heels clicked on the tile, echoed off the walls. She stopped when she got real close. Not touching, but almost.

"You're gorgeous," he said.

"You're not exactly chopped liver."

He laughed again. "Nicest thing anyone's said about me in ages."

"I find using the food groups for compliments has a calming effect."

"Hmm. So when I say your breasts are like ripe melons?"

She grinned. "I get all soft and mushy inside."

He cupped said breasts, enjoying the weight of them in his palms, the contrast of the rigid nipples. "And if I said you taste like sweet cream and honey?"

She sighed. "If you said that," she ran her hands over his chest, "you could probably have your way with me."

"I could?"

She nodded. Looked up at him from behind lowered lashes.

That was it. Enough teasing. He moved to her side and scooped her up in his arms. She didn't feel heavy, and part of that was undoubtedly adrenaline, but he didn't care. Her surprised cry flew around the room as he took the short journey to the steps of the pool. He pushed off her high heels just before he stepped into the water. It was warm, as he'd known it would be. Too warm for him, normally, but tonight, with Tess, it was perfect.

"Swimming?" she said, her hands a bit tight around his neck."

"Well, sure. I thought we'd do laps. I'm sure there's a stopwatch around here somewhere."

Her smile. Damn, what it did to him.

"It is warm, right?"

He took two steps down, and lowered her backside just below the surface of the water. "As a bath."

She gasped, arching up. "So I see."

"But you're not going in the water."

"I'm not?"

He shook his head as he walked her over to the side of the pool adjacent to the whirlpool. He set her down carefully so that her legs dipped in the pool. At the perfect height, the water lapped at her gently, teasing the soft cleft between her legs. Which, now that he thought about it, was his job.

He got comfortable, ducking down in the pool, until he could kiss the inside of Tess's knee. The debate now was whether to linger, to go slowly, to make her crazy with lust, or to prevent his own imminent heart failure and just eat her up like a ripe peach.

When she spread her knees and scooted forward, he decided to split the difference. He closed his eyes and licked the soft skin of her inner thigh.

He thought, not for the first time, that life was very, very kind.

TESS GRIPPED THE SIDE OF the pool, praying she wouldn't fall back, hit her head and drown. It would be such an embarrassing way to die. But if he kept nibbling on her inner thigh, she knew she was going to pass out from pure bliss.

The water kept sneaking up on her. Touching her gently just at the right spot. It was like a really big tongue. A companion tongue, if you will, to the exceptionally talented mouth of Dash Black.

This was the right decision. Maybe the best decision she'd ever made. They should do a special about this decision on PBS. It was every late-night fantasy come to life. Every dream, every wish, every wicked, vibrator-induced lust-addled thought that had crossed her mind. And then some.

He kissed the crease where thigh met torso. No one kissed that. She hardly thought of it as a body part. Until this moment. Until he licked along the edge, almost touching her lips, but not quite. He was a madman, a fiend, and she wanted this to last forever.

He chuckled, his vibrations adding a grace note to the tableau. "What?" she asked.

"You," he said, his hot breath fanning her moist flesh.

"Me?"

"The way you moan. It makes me nuts."

"I'm moaning?"

He laughed. "Uh, yeah."

"Then I must be having a good time."

"Must be." He kissed her, moving just a smidge to his right. "I'm glad I'm not the only one."

"Oh, God," she said, as she felt his lips on the edge of her sex.

Then it was gone. "Is something wrong?"

"No."

He smiled slyly. "Just checking." Then he kissed her again, a millimeter closer to her aching clitoris.

"Oh, God!"

He pulled back. "Still okay?"

"Yes," she said, her frustration making the word come out like a shot.

"All right," he said, dragging out the words. "If you have something you want to tell me, I'm right here."

"Gee, thanks. Now, uh, weren't you doing something?"

"Hmm? Oh, yeah." The tip of his tongue, made pointy and hard, touched her where her flesh met tile, then ran straight up until he reached her swollen bud.

She gasped, moaned, gripped the sides of the pool with all her strength. His tongue flicked once, twice... Dammit she was close. This close. And then...gone. Gone!

Tess jerked her back straight, her eyes flew open in outrage. "What?"

He looked up at her with a smug half smile. "Yes?"

"What do you think you're doing?"

"I'm not sure what you mean."

"You've got to be kidding."

"Pardon?"

She released her death grip on the edge of the pool and grabbed him by his hair. "Dash Black, are you insane or just a sadist?"

His wide, innocent eyes blinked at her as if she'd lost her marbles. Then he opened his mouth, but stopped midword. He smiled. "I'm definitely insane," he said. "And clearly a sadist. But a very short-term sadist."

"You're teasing me."

He nodded, wincing a bit as she tightened her grip.

"Remember what I said a little while ago? About you having your way with me?"

He nodded again.

"I was teasing."

"Oh, no you weren't."

She pushed him back just far enough to clamp her knees tightly together. "Oh, no?"

In one graceful movement, he'd bolstered himself up with his arms, then twisted on the side of the pool beside her. Once he was seated, he turned to her with a puppy dog look. "Please, may I have my way with you?"

"No. The window of opportunity has passed."

"Can't we open a new window."

She crossed her arms over her chest, and turned her back. "Sorry. The offer was only good up to two minutes ago."

"Are you sure?"

She felt his hands on her shoulders, then his lips on the back of her neck. She tried to hide her shiver. "I'm absolutely sure. And don't think you can get me to change my mind just by..."

"Just by what?"

His tongue teased her ear. Swirled around the shell, then dipped inside, giving her goose bumps goose bumps. "By doing that."

"This?" he whispered. "This is nothing. No offense to your ear or anything, but there's just not that much to work with."

"You seem to be doing pretty well."

"Now, there is a place, and yes, it's somewhere on your body, where my true talents could shine."

She turned abruptly, staring him straight in the eyes. "My...feet?"

He shook his head.

"My elbow?"

He frowned. "Jeez, not even close."

"What about here?" she asked, touching the tip of her finger to her lips.

"Much warmer." He kissed her, right where she'd pointed. It started off gently, then his tongue plunged inside and swept across her palate. He kissed her and kissed her and did things that had never been done before, and she couldn't have explained what those things were on pain of death, but she never wanted him to stop. Well, until she had to breathe, or die. She gasped, opened her eyes, and saw that whatever he'd done, it had been good for him, too.

"Wow," he said.

"Yeah."

"And that's not even the good body part."

"Dash?"

"Yeah?"

"I'm going to count to five."

He tilted his head a bit to the side. "And?"

"And at the end of five, a second window of opportunity will have closed."

"Uh-oh."

She smiled. "One..."

He hit the water with a splash, grabbed her knees with his hands and spread her wide. Then he found the perfect body part. She not only forgot to count, she forgot what numbers were.

DASH HAD TO HOLD ON TO her tightly. Her wiggling, while letting him know he was doing a good job, was a bit frightening. The last thing he wanted was for Tess to fall and hurt herself. The good thing was, she was so focused on her body that she didn't have a bit of self-consciousness. Her moans echoed off the walls and swirled inside his brain. It was everything he could do to continue his lavish attention to her clitoris and not just pull her into his arms so he could make love with her till they both drowned.

He wanted her to come. He wanted to taste her when she came, he wanted to hear her cries, he wanted to see that lovely pink blush on her breasts, and he wanted to make sure that she never, ever forgot this night. He wouldn't.

He stopped the slow circles with his tongue, caught the little bud gently between his teeth and flicked at the sensitive flesh. Her hands held his head steady, not that he was going anywhere. Her cries got louder and her whole body started to vibrate. He felt her muscles tense. It was the homestretch.

He focused. Nothing else existed in the world except where the two bodies met. Her taste excited him as much as her gasping breaths. Then her legs came together, trapping him in that most intimate triangle, and a moment later, she spasmed.

He kept licking, kept flicking, as she bucked against him. He might suffocate, but that seemed a small price to pay. The only problem was that he couldn't see her face.

Instead of the quick action he'd been using to get her here, he switched to long, slow strokes with his tongue. Soothing, calming. It worked. The death grip eased from his head, and he was able to take in several much needed breaths. Her cries became whimpers, and then she tugged his hair, wanting him to stop.

He did as she asked, but at the same time he reached behind her and pulled her into the pool. She landed with almost no splash and hooked her arms around his neck.

"Oh, my God," she said.

"Yes, indeed." He smiled at her flushed face, her half-closed eyelids, her moist lips. Irresistibly drawn, he kissed her and when he felt her tongue sneak between his lips, he nearly came right there.

As he reached down to touch her, he remembered the condom in his pocket. Shit. He broke the kiss. "Wait right here. Don't go anywhere."

She nodded, still breathing heavily.

He made it out of the pool in two shakes, terribly conscious of his hardened state as he hurried over to his pants. With wet, sloppy fingers, he found his wallet, pulled out both packets, then dove back in the water so he could swim over to her. He took a second to kiss her breast, then he stood, inches away from the object of his desire.

With one quick rip, he had the package open and then he unrolled the condom over his penis. He said a small prayer of thanks to the inventors of prelubricated rubbers, then his attention went back where it belonged. To the luscious Tess.

He kissed her once more as he reached down between her legs. His fingers teased her for a moment, which had the desired effect of making her spread her legs. Making sure she was braced against the side of the pool, he took hold of himself and found her opening.

The first second of insertion made him groan with pleasure. The second second was even better. "Oh, my God," he whispered.

Tess closed her eyes and leaned her head back as she felt him slip inside her. The warmth, the water, the feel of his slick body against hers, and most especially the faint tremors of her orgasm combined into a heady cocktail of pure pleasure.

She pushed down, wanting him to fill her completely.

"Tess. Oh, dammit. You feel…"

"I know," she said, and then she found his lips. They kissed as he moved slowly in and out of her, making her his own, igniting little fires in her body. His hands roamed over her skin, his tongue swirled and his thick hard cock drove her to the edge of sanity.

As his tempo quickened, she moaned into his mouth, held on tighter. Finally, unable to get close enough this way, she wrapped her legs around his waist and was instantly rewarded with a thrust that made her cry out.

He laughed, but the sound soon turned into a growl as she felt him tense. Another few seconds, and he reared his head back, grimacing in that moment of pleasure so acute it was almost pain.

She trembled with her own climax, clung to him for dear life. He thrust once, twice, again, and then his whole body relaxed. She let go of him with her legs, but it took a second to get her balance. When she did, she found him looking at her with a puzzled expression. "What?"

He shook his head slowly. "Good grief."

She grinned. "Good grief?"

"Yeah. I'd even go so far as to say holy cow."

She couldn't help laughing. The incongruity of this man saying those things. She had no idea he was so funny. Charming, yes. Sexy, oh, baby. But funny had been a surprise. A terrific one. "Don't forget the ever popular, oh, wow."

He kissed the tip of her nose. "Oh, wow."

"Did I tell you yet what a good time I'm having?"

"Yeah."

"Well, I'm telling you again."

"You are very welcome."

"Do you suppose anyone's wondering where we are?"

"Don't know. Don't care."

"Normally, I wouldn't give a damn, either. But with Lacey on the loose, nothing seems safe."

His expression changed. So quickly, in fact, and so dramatically, she needed to clutch his arms so she didn't sink down. "Dash, what is it? Lacey did something, didn't she?"

"It's all right—"

"What's all right? What happened?"

"It's nothing serious. Cullen doesn't let anyone's opinion sway him."

"Oh, God. Cullen? She was talking to him about me? Oh, great. That's just swell. I might as well pack up and go home tonight."

"She's not going to sabotage your business, Tess. I promise you. Not while I have anything to say about it."

Tess let go of him, and stepped back, suddenly chilled despite the warmth of the water. "I need to get back, Dash."

"Tess, don't—"

She held up her hand. "I appreciate you trying to protect me. I do. I know it was meant in kindness. But I didn't have all the facts, Dash. I didn't know my options."

He looked stricken, and she felt badly, but this was her life. Her future. "I'm sorry. I didn't think it through."

She wrapped her arms across her breasts. "Do you know where they keep the towels?"

9

_____

Dash got two towels from the stack in the cabana. When he walked back to Tess, she was already out of the pool. Wet, shiny, beautiful, she had her arms wrapped tightly around her chest, and watching her shiver made him feel like a real jackass.

It wasn't like him. One thing he knew how to do was schmooze. Network. Grease the wheels. He'd rarely, if ever, steered a friend in the wrong direction, and he certainly never endorsed anything he didn't believe in unequivocally. It still bothered him that Cullen had listened to any of Lacey's bullshit. She was a conniver, that one. Tess had every reason to worry. He'd been foolish not to warn her. Not that he still didn't believe he could fix things, but Tess had a right to know.

What bothered him more was that he might have stoked the flames by bringing her out here. All he'd been thinking about was his own pleasure, and showing her a good time. And, as always in the last dozen years, showing a woman a good time meant having sex.

Fool that he was, he hadn't stopped to consider what Cullen might think of a lengthy disappearance.

He wrapped the towel around Tess, and pulled her close, rubbing her back to dry her, as well as comfort her. He felt the strain between them. After such a perfect encounter, too, dammit. He'd make sure Cullen knew the truth about Tess, if it was the last thing he did.

"We'd better get dressed," she said.

He nodded, then went and picked up her clothes. She didn't even look at him as she took them, and pulled the dress over her head. Then she turned her back to slip on her panties.

He finished drying himself, then put on his tux. It felt odd to be dressed like this again. He'd have been much more comfortable in his blue robe, leading Tess to his bed.

Shit, he shouldn't have done this. Selfish prick. He didn't deserve someone like Tess. If Cullen did back out, Dash would finance her flower shop himself.

"My purse?"

He helped her look for the small bag, which turned up on the counter by the fountain. She extracted a small mirror and some lipstick, and fixed herself up. Although she didn't need to do a thing, as far as he was concerned.

She reminded him of a cross between Angelina Jolie and Gina Davis. Nothing ordinary about her looks. She had strong angles, thick, moist lips, huge eyes. She'd never be mistaken for anyone else, and once seen, she would be impossible to forget.

He wanted to kiss her again. Hell, he wanted to take that dress off her, and go for round two. But then, life was full of disappointments. He'd survive. But be the sorrier for missing out. At least he'd tasted her. That was something.

"Come on," he said. "Let's go find Cullen. Let's make sure everything's okay."

She smiled at him, although it didn't reach her eyes. "Okay. I think I could use something a little more potent than champagne."

Slipping his arm around her shoulder, he gave her a little squeeze, then met her gaze. "This was extraordinary," he said. "In the true sense of the word. You're incredibly beautiful, and I can't believe how lucky I am to be here with you."

She glanced away. "Oh, please."

He lifted her chin. "I'm not kidding. I wish…"

"What?"

"I wish I could pursue this."

The gentle, slightly embarrassed smile that had teased her lips vanished with his words. He was really batting a thousand tonight. "I mean it. If things were different—"

"It's okay. I wasn't expecting anything, honest. I know you could never be with someone like me."

"Whoa, wait a minute."

She shook her head. "You know what I'm saying. I'm not in your world, and that's okay. Tonight has been like a fairy tale." She leaned over and kissed him softly on the lips. "Thank you."

"Don't thank me until the deal is done with Cullen."

"No. I'll thank you right now. Whatever happens with Cullen, you've been great. Way above and beyond the call of duty."

"So you're not sorry?"

Her eyes widened. "For what? For a stunning evening? For a sweet, wonderful moment with the mermaid? Oh, no. I'm not sorry.''

He kissed her again, taking his time. Liking her. A lot. He'd remember her taste, her scent, her smile. The way she threw her head back as she came. The thrum of her thighs as the muscles grew taut.

Shit, if he didn't stop right now, he'd be in trouble. He pulled back. ''They're going to call out the hounds if we don't get back.''

''I'm ready.''

''You are. For anything. You watch, Ms. Norton. You're gonna have Cullen eating out of your hand.''

CULLEN WAS EATING OUT OF someone's hand—literally—and it wasn't Tess's. Lacey laughed in that nasally way that made Tess's skin crawl as she fed the older man a canapé. Brad slumped nearby, staring at some brunette's ass as if it were a Monet and he was an art student.

Tess didn't even slow down. She kept on going till she got to the bar. Thankfully, there were only two people in line in front of her. She turned to Dash. ''I'm getting a vodka. Neat. What would you like?''

He grimaced. ''Are you sure?''

She nodded. ''Oh, yeah.''

''I'll have one, too, then. Can't have you going to the happy place alone.''

She grinned. ''Oh, I think the happy place is already pretty crowded. Take Cullen, for example. He's about as happy as a man can be without holding the remote.''

Dash laughed. ''I'll admit, he looks six or seven sheets to the wind. But he'll be sober eventually.''

"Just not tonight."

"No. That ship has definitely sailed." Dash touched her waist with his fingertips as they moved in on the bar.

Tess felt the electrical pulse all the way to her toes. She truly needed a drink. Normally, she was a lightweight, and barely finished a beer. But tonight she could drink her weight in vodka.

Too much sensory input, that's what it was. Being with Dash, and by that she meant in the biblical sense, was enough to make her gibber like an idiot, but add in the magnanimous and lovely Lacey, add a soupçon of Brad, then stir in the fate of her entire future, and she was surprised she hadn't passed out cold.

"Tess?"

She looked to her side. Dash appeared to have been speaking to her. Oh, well. "Pardon?"

"Just vodka? Are you sure?"

"A double."

His brow lifted.

"Hey, I'm not driving. Besides, I'm not trying to get drunk. I just want to chill."

"A double vodka will chill you, all right. After the champagne, and the other—"

She held up a hand to stop him. "I appreciate your concern, but truly, I'm fine. If I had a Xanax I'd take it, but I don't, so vodka is the next best thing."

"So be it." He turned to the handsome bartender who was struggling to hide his obvious attraction. Not to her. To Dash. The guy was practically drooling. "Two doubles of your best vodka."

"Yes, sir, Mr. Black."

Dash brought his hand to her shoulder and she al-

lowed herself the tiny luxury of leaning against him.
Take that, hunky bartender. He's with little ol' me.
So what if it's only for tonight. One night was
enough.

God, when she thought about what they'd done in
the pool house. *Mamma mia,* she was going to have
a tale to tell the Eve's Apple girls. They were going
to croak. Even Mary, who had no interest in the celebrities of the world, was impressed with Dash. Once
she found they'd done it...

It probably wasn't the kind of thing to put in the
paper or anything. In fact, she should just keep her
mouth shut. What they'd done was private. Personal.

Yeah, like that was going to happen.

"Here you go."

She took her drink, clinked the glass against his.
"Na zdrovie."

"Skoal."

They tossed the clear liquid back, and Tess only
choked for a few minutes. Once the coughing
stopped, she felt much better.

"So now what?" Dash asked, leading her away
from the bar and the hungry gaze of Chad or Justin
or whatever the young man's name was.

"Hmm. Usually at parties like this I like to start a
conga line."

"Could be interesting."

"Or there's always charades. Everyone could play,
although we'd be up most of the night writing down
five hundred movie titles."

Dash shook his head. "No. Too many bad sports.
If they don't win, they tend to close banks and ruin
small countries."

"Definitely not charades."

"Dancing?"

"Not yet. I'm still absorbing the alcohol."

"A seat in the corner so we can watch people?"

"As long as we get to say rude things about them, I'm your gal."

"Very well." He looked past her, then to the right. "You stay here where I can find you. I'll go get us the perfect table for saying rude things."

"Excellent."

He kissed the tip of her nose, then headed south. He'd parked her near one of the dessert tables, which was awfully considerate. She grabbed a plate, bone china, of course, and started down the dangerous path of outrageous confections. Chocolate everything, from dipped strawberries to mousses—mice?—called her name, repeatedly, and she tried not to pig out too badly, but jeez, it was like being locked in the Godiva store. No mere mortal could resist.

Except, of course, for all the skinny women. She looked at the people around her. Lots of gorgeously dressed fashion plates, most of them holding liquor, but nary a woman with a dessert anywhere near her. The men didn't seem to be resistant. But the women?

If the price of being a size 0 was no chocolate, forget about it. Life was too short to ignore truffles.

As she plucked something sinful onto her plate, she felt Dash move up behind her. He touched her again, only this time, his fingers sort of jabbed her. She jerked around, and nearly dropped her plate. It wasn't Dash.

"Hey, babe."

"Brad. What are you doing off your leash?" When

he stood close to her like this, she could smell a hint of his Hugo Boss cologne. It was one of the things she'd liked about him.

"Bitter, are we?"

"I'm not bitter. I'm witty." She stepped back, looked at him from more of a distance. The attraction was still there, at least on a physical level. The guy was good looking, sort of a cross between Matt Damon and River Phoenix. His hair, always appearing just mussed, but slaved over with excruciating attention to detail, was perfect. As was his tux. She felt quite certain Brad could have any woman he wanted. And that he probably did.

"Whatever," he said, brushing her comment aside like a gnat. "Come on. Let's dance."

"I don't want to dance with you."

He slid his hand around her waist and tugged at her. "Just this time."

"No."

"You're the one that said we could be friends."

"I lied."

"Tess, baby." He took her plate and put it on the table. "You need to dance with me."

"Why would I need to do that?"

He leaned in close, his breath more whisky than oxygen. "Because you need Lacey to lay off."

Tess stiffened and tried to break free from his grasp. "Cut it out, Brad. I don't want to do this."

"I can fix things for you. I know Cullen better than Lacey."

"I don't need your help."

"Yes you do, sweetheart. And all you have to do is play nice."

"Play nice? What does that mean? Sleep with you?"

"I don't have any interest in sleeping."

"Brad, knock it off. Now."

He chuckled, his eyes narrowing unpleasantly. "It's no skin off my teeth if you want to move back to Tinyville. You're the one that wants the flower shop."

"Not if being with you is the price I have to pay for it."

He leaned in, so his lips were right next to her ear. "You wanted to play in the big leagues, honey. It's not like it would be the first time. And if you want to put up a fight, all the better for me."

"If she doesn't want to, I do."

Tess jerked back again to see Dash standing right behind Brad, looking like he was seconds away from smashing Brad's face in. Which pissed her off even more. What is it with men? "It's okay, Dash. Brad was just leaving."

"You got that right."

Brad let her go, then held up both hands in a conciliatory gesture. "Whoa, back off, man. I didn't know you two were an item."

"Whether we're an item or not is immaterial," Dash said. "The lady said no."

Brad ran a hand through his hair, then gave Dash a crooked grin. "The lady has said no before when she meant yes."

Dash's face got redder as he moved in on Brad. "She means no right now."

Tess felt her own temperature rise. "*She* is right here. *She* is perfectly capable of handling herself. *She* is walking away from this nonsense.'' She turned to Brad, and got close to his face. ''Grow up. You're not a child anymore.'' Then she turned on Dash. ''I know your intentions are honorable, but I don't need you to ride to my rescue. I can take care of myself. You're not going to be around to play the hero after tonight.''

She stepped back, took a deep breath then let it go. ''If you'll excuse me, I'm going to the powder room.'' With what she hoped was an air of dignity, she threw her head back, then headed toward the bathrooms.

The band played something vaguely familiar and slightly sad, and her bravura slipped away with each step. Brad's slimy proposal still clung to her like sour musk while another uncomfortable thought made her feel even worse. She had sex with Dash, while he'd done her a huge favor. Wasn't that exactly what Brad had just suggested?

She walked into the ladies' room, disappointed to see how crowded it was. Being alone would be good. On the other hand, maybe thinking too much was just asking for trouble.

When a stall opened up, she locked herself inside, then sat down on the commode. What had she done? Why hadn't she listened to her own advice, and kept her clothes on?

She'd been so excited that Dash Black wanted her that she'd gone back on every decision she'd struggled so hard to make. He was a man *not* to do. Operative word ''not.'' So what had she done? Did him. First night. Only night. Perfect. Her mother would be so proud.

She groaned as she put her head in her hands. How could she be so bright about work and so stupid when it came to men? What would it take for her to get her act together?

At least she wouldn't have to worry about seeing Dash again. And one night, while it may not be her finest hour, wasn't going to kill her. But she swore, right there, that she would never, never put herself in this position again. She remembered an episode of *Seinfeld* where George decided the only hope he had was to figure out the best possible plan of attack, then do the opposite. If he was attracted to a woman, he gave it a pass. If he wasn't, he'd go for it. If his heart said no, his mouth said yes.

That was going to be her new philosophy in life. When it came to men, the last person she'd listen to was herself. If she felt drawn to a man, she'd run like hell.

Whenever she had doubts about this brilliant new plan, she'd remember Brad. How flattered she'd been when he'd flirted with her at the AIDS benefit at the Guggenheim. How elated she'd been when he'd asked her out. How dumbstruck she'd been when she realized he was one of the wealthiest men in New York. How devastated she'd been when she realized he'd only dated her because she was one step above complete boredom.

Okay, then. No more trusting her instincts. Ever.

That settled, she finished up her business, ran a quick hand through her hair, and walked out to face life on new terms.

Only, as she got closer to Dash, as she watched the group of gorgeous women fawning over him, laughing at whatever witty thing he'd said, her resolve wobbled. God, he was too gorgeous for words. And now she knew what he looked like without the tux. The memory slowed her down, and she grabbed onto the nearest chair to steady herself.

She'd made love with Dash Black. Her. She had. She knew, because she'd been there. For the rest of her life, she could remember it whenever she wanted to. In the pool with the mermaid. In the middle of the night. When the band played in the main house. And no one was the wiser.

Screw it. If it was a mistake, so be it. She wasn't going to diminish the experience. It was a once in a lifetime. She could live with that.

She headed for him, calmer, even as her heart beat faster. When he caught sight of her, he smiled in such a way that it took her very breath. He must have excused himself, because the women stepped back, gave him space to walk away.

And walk away he did. Right smack dab in front of Tess. Close enough for his arms to go around her waist. Close enough to press his body against hers. Close enough for a kiss so sweet, so thorough, so bone-melting, that she knew, beyond all shadow of a doubt that she was a goner.

10

DASH HELD HER TIGHTER than he should. Kissed her as if it was his last kiss. Which it probably was. The night had begun as a lark, and had turned into something he didn't understand and wasn't comfortable with. Especially this feeling of protectiveness toward Tess.

Reluctantly, he broke the kiss, looked deeply into her dark, lovely eyes. "Dance with me," he whispered. "One last dance before we head home."

She nodded, let him lead her to the dance floor, and then she put her head on his shoulder while he circled her with his arms. They moved slowly, weaving together, him rubbing her bare back, wallowing in the softness of her skin. When she sighed, he let himself relax a bit. Damn, but she felt good.

She was right, of course. She was strong and self-sufficient, and he hardly knew her, so why did he want so badly to make things right for her?

It wasn't hard to figure out his reactions to Brad. Tess was well rid of that bastard. Brad belonged to that breed of wealthy wastrels who figured money could buy everything, especially women. Dash knew of two particularly messy affairs that ended in abortion and payoffs. Both girls, and they had barely been over eighteen, had been employees, working for

Brad's family business. Both had left town abruptly for who knows what future.

On the other hand, Brad wasn't unremittingly bad. His family had made a fortune in telecommunications, and Brad had a real talent for restructuring mergers. He worked hard, and he'd been known to go the extra mile to save jobs. Dash had first met Brad at the Noir Gala, and Brad had donated a pretty penny, all anonymously.

Lacey, too, had her moments. She could be generous and she put a lot of energy into the New York art scene. The problem with both of them was selfishness.

Dash had to admit, he suffered from the same malady. When you're given everything, it's easy to think you deserve everything.

He touched the back of Tess's neck, once again drowning in her warm, soft skin. She looked up at him, smiling, then snuggled back to the crook of his shoulder. Was it possible he deserved her? Dammit, he hoped so. But not because he had money or power. Because he liked her. A lot. More than he'd counted on, that's for sure. She'd done something no other woman had. She'd made him want to play his music for her.

He'd never wanted anyone to share that part of himself. His music, mostly classical played on his baby grand in the back room of his penthouse, was the most personal part of his life.

He'd studied for years, having discovered a natural ability when he was nine. He composed his first piece at eighteen, a dreadful rip-off of a Bach étude, but it had started him on his lifelong love of composing.

As the years went by, and he lost more and more of his privacy, he'd kept his music close to the vest. His father and Patrick knew he played, but they didn't understand. Dash didn't want them to. It was his.

In all those years, two women had heard him. Neither time planned. Sandy had surprised him at three in the morning. A nice girl, beautiful and bright, he'd left her sleeping in his bed. She'd stood at the door to the music room, he was never sure how long. After he'd finished, she'd clapped. He'd nearly jumped out of his skin. She'd wanted to hear more, but he'd deflected her, and they'd gone back to bed.

The only other woman to hear his music was Julia. It was better with her. She'd discovered him, like Sandy, when he thought she was asleep. But when she'd poked her head in, she'd evidently seen he hadn't wanted to be disturbed, and she'd left. She never asked him about it, which was another reason he liked her. He'd thought, for a while, that the two of them might have a future together, but in the end, their lives were impossible to mesh. With her acting jobs all over the map and his work for Noir, they rarely ended up in the same city, let alone the same bed. But they were friends, and he'd been there for her when the whole Benjamin thing had gone down.

And now there was this girl. Woman. Tess, who wasn't famous, who had no public demands on her time. Beautiful Tess who wanted so very much to be strong and do things her way.

Maybe that was it. Why he felt such a pull toward her. He liked her spirit, her abandon. But he also respected the fact that she had concrete goals and the chutzpah to follow through.

On the other hand, he might just be crazy about her lips.

The thought spurred him into action, and he lifted her chin so he could taste her again. His eyes closed and his feet stopped, but the swaying didn't. Holding her close, her scent, now infused with a hint of chlorine, was actually rather exciting. More than likely, he'd never be around a pool again without thinking of Tess.

"It's late," he said. "And there are too many people here."

Her gaze shifted as her cheeks pinked. "Dash..."

"I'm not suggesting we go back to the pool. But perhaps we should think about going home."

She nodded. "That's a pretty good idea."

"Unless you want to stay here. They have guest cottages. You saw them. I'm sure it would be no problem."

"No, but thanks. It's past midnight, and even though the carriage hasn't turned back into a pumpkin, I'm rapidly losing my fairy dust."

He stepped back as the song ended. "Anything you need to do before we get the car?"

"One thing. I need to speak to Cullen."

"Okay," he said, scanning the group at the nearest bar.

"Alone."

He looked back at Tess. "Of course. I'm sorry for my interference tonight. It wasn't my best performance."

"I appreciate everything you've done, Dash. But this is my ball game, and only I can step up to the plate."

"Fair enough. I'll go see about the car. You go hit a homer."

"At this point, I'd settle for not striking out."

He kissed the tip of her nose, wanting to do far more. Instead, he winked, then headed toward the ballroom doors.

In a few hours, he'd drop her off at her place. She'd go back to being the plant lady, and he'd go back to being the Noir poster boy. Damn pity the two couldn't mix.

He stepped into the foyer, dismayed at the length of the valet line. Even more distressing was the gaggle of young females heading his way, their bleached smiles and button noses uniformly perfect. If he hurried, he could make it out the door before they caught him, but then Tess wouldn't know where to find him. No, he'd stay. Be charming as hell, flirt a little, laugh at foolish jokes. It was, after all, his job.

TESS HAD ABSOLUTELY NO idea what she'd said to Cullen. At least he'd been by himself when she'd approached, and he'd been a little stiff when she'd stuck out her hand. He'd looked at her for a long time, and when she said she hoped they'd be speaking soon, he'd nodded. Even managed a bit of a smile.

Why Lacey had it out for her was anyone's guess. Tess had never done anything to her. Not really. But then, even their first meeting had been tense.

Brad had taken Tess to an art gallery opening. It was their second date. He'd introduced her to Lacey, who was the sponsor of the artist, and then Lacey had grabbed Brad's hand and led him to a sculpture. He'd come back for Tess, and she'd noticed that Lacey seemed a bit miffed. Tess hadn't given it another thought. But every time she'd run into Lacey, there had been friction.

Tess wound her way through the dwindling crowd, anxious to find Dash. As nervous as she'd been about going out with him, it felt a little odd to seek him out for familiarity and comfort.

She found him standing in a makeshift line in the foyer. Surrounded, of course, by a bevy of beauties. She slowed, then came to a stop watching the interactions. Mostly, watching Dash pour on the charm.

He did it effortlessly. Even though she couldn't hear what was being said, she could see him shift his attention from one woman to the next, leaving no one out in the cold. He leaned in, smiled, mirrored their behavior, and the women ate it up with a spoon.

Was it inbred? Or was his savoir faire a result of years of training? She imagined it was a combination of both. What she also imagined was that Dash being charming was like Dash breathing. Nothing he could do about it. If he was with a woman, he was a dazzler.

Which meant, of course, that her spectacular night wasn't quite as spectacular as she would have hoped. She didn't think she was a pity fuck or anything, but she was just one of many. One of the vast number of women within Dash's orbit. That he made her feel so special was exactly the point. He did, because he could. It was a gift, and a damn good one for a man in his position.

No wonder the most fabulous women in the world wanted Dash as their escort. Who wouldn't? The miracle was that she, little old Tess from Tinyville, as Brad had so eloquently put it, had been treated to a privileged view. Up close and personal. About as personal as it gets, actually.

Every woman currently hanging on to Dash's every word would have traded a great deal to be in Tess's shoes tonight. Or out of them, as the case may be.

All in all, she had the distinct impression that she'd look back on tonight as something extraordinary. Wild, unpredictable, a regular roller coaster, but something she wouldn't regret. She'd been a princess for one night. That was as much as anyone had a right to ask for.

She headed toward him, a mixture of ennui and exhaustion making her want to collapse into the nearest chair. Instead, she held her head up high, just like Ms. Tulley had taught her in sixth grade deportment class. If she'd had a book, she could have put it on her head and walked the length of the mansion. Thank God she didn't have a book.

She giggled as she stepped into the circle of women surrounding Dash. He turned to her immediately, and his grin warmed her from her toes up. A perfect example of what she'd been thinking about. The man was charisma personified.

"I was about to go look for you," he said, as he took hold of her hand and pulled her next to him. "But I would have lost my place in line."

"Hmm," she said, leaning a little against his shoulder. "I never really thought about it, but who are the VIPs when everyone is a VIP?"

"I think they rank in order of power first, money second." He turned to a petite redhead with a fetching overbite who hovered to his right. "What do you think, Toni? You've been around this kind of thing since birth.''

"It depends," she said, shifting her attention between Dash and Tess. "This kind of shindig is pretty egalitarian. There are a few folks who stand above the rest, but not that many.''

"Who?" Tess asked.

"The Spielbergs." Toni rolled her eyes. "Even here, Hollywood still holds court. Then there's Eleanor Pratchett, who gets about anything her little heart desires, due to the simple fact that she's the fourth richest woman in the world.''

"That would do it, all right," Tess said.

Toni gave her a mischievous grin. "Now Dash here, he's right up there at the top.''

"Whoa," he said, holding out his hand to stop her. "I'm not even close to the top of this pyramid.''

"Oh, but you are." She looked from Tess to the woman beside her, a tall blonde in a dazzling dress. "You know what I mean, don't you, Kate?''

"Absolutely. Dash has the kind of magic that can't be bought or brokered. He's a golden boy, and he'll be a golden boy for the rest of his life.''

"Explain that," Tess said, wondering why she couldn't have met women like these instead of the Laceys of the world.

"Clearly," Toni said, "he's gorgeous. But that's not enough.''

"Hey, wait just a minute here." Dash frowned, which just made him look even more handsome. "You can't talk about me like I'm someone's prize pony. I'm right here, for God's sake.''

Kate waved his argument away. "Shush. This is

important sociological research. Be quiet in the name of science.''

''Science?''

''And he's got the lure of the Noir empire behind him,'' Tess went on. ''There's power there, and money, although nothing compared to half the room, so it's a piece of the puzzle, not the solution.''

''It's his TV.''

''What's that?''

''It's a survey done by Marketing Evaluations to rate awareness. Usually it's about movie stars, but anyone in the public eye has a Q score. And I would imagine Dash's number is right at or near the top. Everyone knows who you are, darling,'' Kate said, smiling. ''I can't picture a place in the world where you wouldn't be recognized.''

''How about this line,'' Dash said.

They laughed, and Tess squeezed his hand. This was a perfect way to end the evening. She'd been completely ready to be snubbed when she'd walked into this little group, and she'd been dead wrong. Kate and Toni, at least, were nice. Genuine. If she'd been part of the inner circle, she'd have pursued a friendship.

But she wasn't. Whether they were as nasty as Lacey or as nice as these two, they were still *them* not *us*. She was the opposite of Dash. Her Q rating was zero, and would remain that way. She was damn lucky they let her water the plants.

''Can we talk about something else, please?'' Dash asked. ''Anything else?''

''Sure,'' Kate said. ''How about you introduce us to your lady friend?''

Dash groaned. "Charisma, maybe, but social graces? Not a one. Pardon me, please. This exquisite creature is Tess Norton."

After brief introductions all around, Dash pulled her close and put his arm around her shoulder.

"How did you two meet, Tess?" Toni asked.

Tess's stomach tightened, and she felt her cheeks heat. Which pissed her off, because she wasn't ashamed of who she was. At least, she hadn't thought she was.

"Tess is a wizard with plants. Gardens. The whole spectrum of growing things."

"Really?" Kate's perfectly arched brow rose. "I dabble a bit in orchids."

"I know a few things about orchids," Tess said. "Enough to know it takes a great deal of patience to grow them."

"When I say I dabble, I really mean my gardener dabbles. I wouldn't know which end to plant."

"That's why we have gardeners," Toni said. "To do the grunt work so we can take all the glory."

Tess's smile froze. The grunt work. That's exactly what she did. She didn't dabble, she dug with her hands. With her short, stubby little nails. And she lived in an apartment that cost less than Dash Black's monthly fresh flower budget.

"Is that the door?" Dash pulled her forward, keeping his hold tight. "Did we actually make it to the front of the line? I believe we did." He bowed to his friends. "Good night all you lovelies. Try not to break too many hearts."

Then they were outside, and Dash's limo door was being opened. She scooted inside and Dash followed.

Once the door was closed, she felt a sense of tremendous relief. It was damn hard being a princess, even for one night. There was the prince to deal with, and wicked members of the court, jesters and fools. She'd be glad to get back to her shoebox apartment. The only thing she would miss about this whole experience was Dash.

She'd see him, of course, but it wouldn't be like this. She'd be his plant lady, and pretty soon, he'd forget he even took her to this party. For him, it was just another social obligation. And she was just another woman to charm.

"What's wrong?"

She realized she was frowning and stopped it. "Tired."

"Big doings."

"I'll say."

"Lots of imbibing."

"Some might say too much."

He shook his head. "Naw. We're not driving."

"True."

His smile faded, and his eyes grew serious. "I had an incredible time tonight."

"Me, too."

"Really? Despite my meddling?"

"It's okay. I'm not worried. Besides, if something does go wrong, it's not going to be because of you."

"I'd still like to help."

"You have." She leaned over and kissed him gently on the lips. "You've been wonderful."

He put his arm around her shoulder and pulled her close. Her head fit perfectly on the crook of his neck, and she relaxed into his arms. He felt so solid, so real like this. For another two hours she'd let her worries go. They'd all be waiting for her on her doorstep.

He rubbed her arm, so softly it was almost a tickle. It felt like heaven.

"You did everything right, you know."

"Hmm?"

"Tonight. You were great. With Cullen, with Brad. With me. You're pretty special."

"Yeah, I'm a peach."

He squeezed her arm. "You are. I was the luckiest man there."

She opened her mouth for a smart remark, but changed her mind. "Thank you."

"You're welcome."

She sighed as she curled her hand beneath her chin and closed her eyes. She didn't want to sleep. Just to listen to his heartbeat, to smell his scent. To memorize the feel of his fingers.

When she got home, she'd write to her friends. Give them a recap. Get their opinions. Although she knew exactly what she had to do. Forget about being with Dash Black, because that wasn't going to happen. Take action on her battle plan, not just think about it. Start investigating different funding sources, just in case.

Her life was full, rich, good. She should be on top of the world. And she definitely shouldn't be thinking a man was going to rescue her. She didn't need rescuing, so why did she feel this way? Maybe because when life was good, it felt a million times better to have someone to share it with.

Someone to snuggle up to in bed. To laugh with at private jokes. She wanted a man to love her as much as she would love him. A partnership. None of which was going to happen unless she stopped seeing men like Dash.

Bad move, that. Thinking about Dash was just plain dumb. When you know you can't have what you want, what's the use of wishing?

"Tess?"

"Yes?"

"Are you falling asleep?"

"No."

He lifted her up so she could look into his eyes. "Good," he whispered. Then he kissed her.

11

————————

THE KISS WOKE HER UP. His lips, his talented tongue, his fingers brushing the skin of her arm so lightly it sent shivers down her spine.

She touched the back of his head, holding him steady as she deepened the kiss, her body tingling with anticipation. He nibbled her lower lip, then traced it with the tip of his tongue, only to dip inside once more. He moaned as his hand moved to her breast.

He touched her there, cupped her, and the pleasure shot through her like a lightning bolt. Her head fell back as she gasped. "Oh, God."

"No, just me," he whispered. "And I'm not sharing you with anyone."

Her smile froze as she moved her hand. Something was wrong. Seriously wrong. One nail, long, tapered, manicured, remained on her fingers. One. The rest of her nails were her own damn nails. "Oh, crap," she whispered, sitting up a bit, dislodging his palm.

"What's wrong?"

"My nails."

He sat up straighter then dipped into his pocket. "I'm sure no one noticed," he said. He opened his hand, showing her four plastic nails, which looked rather pitiful. "I found as many as I could."

She looked at her other hand. Two nails, the pinky and thumb, survived on that one.

"Honestly, Tess. It's okay. Everyone was too busy looking at your beautiful face."

His tone made her shift her gaze to him. His brows creased with concern, his lips curved down in a troubled frown. The guy was seriously bummed about her fingernails. It struck her as...

Funny. She giggled. Then she laughed. Hard.

Dash's expression went from concerned to confused, and that made her laugh harder still. Finally, he relaxed and smiled, although he clearly didn't get the humor of the situation.

"They're just nails, Dash," she said after catching her breath.

"I know, but—"

She held up her hand for a moment, then removed the three survivors. "There. So I won't be doing any hand modeling in the near future. Good thing I have the whole plant thing to fall back on."

Dash shook his head. "You're..."

She raised her brows. "Yes?"

"You're something else."

"Is that good?"

He leaned closer, touched her lips for a brief kiss, then whispered, "That's very, very good."

A second later, all thoughts of nails were abandoned for a much more satisfying matter.

THEY PULLED UP TO Tess's apartment, and Dash woke her as gently as he could. She'd been curled up next to him, half on him, really, since they'd crossed over into Manhattan. It had felt damn good.

She smiled up at him, her hair spiky, her cheek indented where it had met his lapel. She yawned, covering her mouth with her hand, then stretched. He watched her with a vivid longing, knowing this was how she would wake up most mornings. It surprised him how much he wanted to be there to see it.

"What time is it?" she asked.

"Almost four."

"Oh, God."

"I know."

"Did you get any rest?"

He shook his head. "I'll go on home and crash. Not much on the docket for tomorrow, except an interview with *Vanity Fair*."

"Yeah," she said. "Me, too. Damn magazines. When will they learn to leave us alone?"

He leaned forward and kissed her lush lips. "Go to bed. Sleep long, sleep well. And thank you. I've had one hell of a good night."

"You're welcome. I had a pretty nice time, too."

"Yeah?"

She nodded, but the sleepy, saucy grin faded. "You were great to do this for me, Dash."

"I thought we'd agreed not to say that anymore."

"We did? Where was I?"

"Maybe I just thought it. It doesn't matter. We can agree right now. No more thanks. I got more out of the evening than you did."

She giggled. "I wouldn't exactly say that."

"You're bad, you know that?"

"Terrible," she whispered.

He leaned forward to kiss her again, but then she yawned, which sort of spoiled the mood.

"Sorry."

"It's okay. Come on. Let's do this before we both fall asleep." He opened his door, and went around to her side of the car, signaling Moe that he could stay put.

Tess dragged herself out, wobbled a bit as she stepped up on the curb, but he was there to steady her. She leaned into him, and they walked slowly to the front of her brownstone.

It was quiet. At least as quiet as it could be in New York. Just the occasional horn, a car alarm several blocks away, and the rumble of the subway as it ran beneath the street. Tess got her key out, and they went inside.

He led her to the stairs, but her hand on his stopped him. "You don't need to walk me up. I'll be fine."

He gave her a look that he hoped would stop her foolishness. It did. She shrugged, and they went up, and up and up. Finally, when he was about ready to send for oxygen, they got to her door. In the dark hallway, Dash pulled her close, although he didn't kiss her. He held her. That's all. He didn't want to let her go. Didn't want this to be their one and only night together. But his options were limited. Terribly limited.

It was time to say goodbye. Not good-night. He'd undoubtedly run into her again, and he hoped they could be friends. Probably not, though. That might be too difficult.

He kissed her cheeks, then the tip of her nose, and finally, gently, kissed her lips.

She backed away first, smiled, then she shrugged. He knew exactly what she meant.

"You need me on that Cullen thing, you call me."

She nodded. "You have any gladiola emergencies, I'm your gal."

"I'd like—"

"What?"

"Nothing. I'm out of here. You be good."

"I'll do my best."

Another heartbeat, another stupid wish, and then he turned, and headed down the hall. Back to his perfect life.

To: Erin and Samantha
From: Tess
Subject: Why I'm A Bonehead

Dear Friends Who Don't Make Fun of The Fatally Stupid,

So, how are you guys doing? I hope the weather is nice and that you're having a good weekend.

Oh, okay. Jeez. I was getting to it.

Last night was the most interesting night of my life. Found out I have an enemy. A rather formidable one, at that. Her name is Lacey, she's rich as Croesus, and she wields her power with an iron fist. She doesn't care for me, shockingly enough, because as we all know, I'm the sweetest goddamn thing this side of the Pecos. Anyway, I spoke to the money man, who seemed very receptive, until Lacey (hereinafter referred to as The Bitch) got hold of him and told him who the hell knows what. Nothing flattering, that's for sure. So I have no idea if I'm going to be a rich and famous plant lady to the stars, or a checker at the Piggly Wiggly on State Street in good old Tulip, Texas.

The odds in Vegas are on the latter.

All RIGHT already.

Dash… Good grief. You'd think he was God's gift to the women of planet earth, the way everyone fawns over him. I don't see it. I mean, he's nice and all, and yes, I'll admit he's good looking, but really. Have these women no shame?

HAHAHAHA! Oh, God, I just crack myself up.

Paparazzi took our pictures. I acted like it was a pain in the ass while I, of course, was so excited I nearly passed out. But that was only a teeny tiny piece of the most incredible night. In fact, I'm going to call you guys and tell you, because I can't stand it. I have to say it in real words and hear you gasp. Okay, I'm selfish. But at least I'm immature. <g> Here's the thing I need to write, so I don't conveniently forget it when I speak to you. It's the moron part. (see subject)

I slept with him. You'll understand when I tell you it was in an indoor pool, with a mermaid painted on the bottom. It was hazy, and warm. It was DASH BLACK. Ergo. I did it.

I'm not sorry, either.

Kinda.

Not sorry really. Just sort of, well, missing him. Thinking about him. All the time. No, you don't understand. ALL. THE. TIME.

I cannot have this man. Is everyone clear on this? I cannot, no matter what, be his babe. He made that abundantly clear, as if I didn't already know that.

However. My pea brain insists on toying with the

notion. Of devising cunning little reasons for me to accidentally run into him in his bedroom, say, or in the shower.

Oh, Dash. I'm sorry. I thought you were a rhododendron that I was going to care for. In the shower. Naked.

So you can see the problem, yes?

Me: Big Dope
Him: Unattainable
Solution:

Phew. I'm so glad I'm asking you guys what to do. I have every confidence that you two will see a crystal clear path to not only solving the problem, but ensuring a long and happy life for me as Mrs. Dash Black. Right? *Right?*

If I have to depend on my own instincts, my own finely honed sense of inner peace, serenity, and the wisdom of my forbearers, I'll be screwed beyond salvation. So please, please, write back soon.

And yes, I'm going to call, too.

Me? Obsessive?

Oh, shut up.

Love you both!
Tess

TESS SHUT OFF her computer, and leaned her head against the back of her chair.

Two days later, and she was still insane. She'd gone to work today, gone to the bank, even managed to roast a chicken in her Easy Bake oven, so she guessed she wasn't certifiably insane. Just insane enough to make her want to weep.

Why, why, why couldn't she get it through her thick skull that her affaire with Dash was over. Done. Kaput. Finito.

It wasn't fair, really. If someone was going to get a chance to go out with (and have sex with) someone like Dash, then that first someone should have, at the very least, the possibility that things could, you know, get serious.

She'd seen him on *E!* tonight. There was a little blip from the party. She hadn't even seen the TV cameras, so obsessed was she with the man of her dreams. But they'd been there, and they'd captured Dash in all his sartorial splendor. Truly. Good camera work, excellent lighting.

She saw her own elbow on the screen for about a tenth of a second, which was absolutely thrilling. She was so delighted that when she saw the teaser, she'd called up all her friends and threatened them with bodily harm if they didn't watch. Talk about bragging rights! Her elbow. Neato.

She sighed. Like she had any right to complain. She'd had her night, she'd gotten exactly what she asked for, and now, like some whiny baby, she wanted more. She wanted her business and Dash.

Dash.

If only he hadn't looked at her with quite so much interest. If he'd been a bad kisser. Better yet, if he'd had one of those unfortunate pencil penises. But noooo. Dash was not only gorgeous, but hung.

She stood up, tired of listening to her own pathetic carping. Something must be done.

She picked up the phone and dialed Mary's number.

"Yo."

"Mary? Come with me to coffee."

"When?"

"Now."

"Okay."

"God, I love you."

"I know. See you in ten."

"'kay."

Tess threw on a different sweater, then ran her fingers through her hair. Makeup? No. Clean teeth? Absolutely. By the time she'd finished spitting, Mary knocked. Tess turned off the bathroom light, grabbed her purse, and swung open the door.

Only it wasn't Mary. She could tell because her heart nearly beat out of her chest, and she forgot how to breathe.

"You were on your way out."

"No. I mean, yes. But it's okay. What are you doing here, Dash?"

He looked at her, his brows drawn, frowning. "I came to see you."

"Oh?" She sounded so casual. Like it was no big deal. Like she wasn't about to melt into a small puddle of pure lust.

He shrugged. On him, it was a move out of a ballet. God, those shoulders. He wore a pale-blue dress shirt, sleeves rolled up to expose manly arms and his silver and gold Rolex. His jeans had that well-worn look that made her want to play with the zipper. Simple. Stunning. Here.

"Look, I should have called. I'm sorry. I—"

"Hey, I didn't know we were going to have a party."

Dash swung around as Tess's gaze went to Mary. Her outfit was a lot more complicated than Dash's. She wore a patchwork denim skirt right out of Woodstock, a T-shirt shouting "Krycek Lives!" and a cardigan that looked like standard issue from Our Lady Of Perpetual Agony. Not to mention her purse, which was large enough to sleep two comfortably.

"You two have plans," Dash said, stepping back in retreat, whether from the situation or Mary's outfit, Tess wasn't sure.

"We're just going to coffee," she said. "Would you like to join us?"

Dash looked a little worried as his gaze moved back and forth between the women. "Coffee?"

"It's a hot beverage," Mary said. "I think you'd like it if you gave it a try."

He smiled. Sort of. "Uh, sure."

"Great," Mary said. "Let's book."

Dash stood very still as Tess locked the door behind her. She could see he was rethinking his decision, so she had to make her move quickly. She took hold of his hand and started down the hall. What she hadn't counted on was the electric thrill she got from touching him. The charge that made her stumble and nearly fall on her behind. But Dash was there to steady her, his arm sliding around her waist.

She nearly swooned.

Swooned. Jesus.

"So, I hear you had a wingding of a time at your little soiree," Mary said, oblivious to the petite drama beside her.

"Wingding?"

"Mary speak," Tess explained. "You'll get the hang of it."

"Wow. Coffee and Mary all in one evening? I don't know if I'm ready."

Mary laughed, then slugged him in the shoulder. "You're okay."

"Thanks. And ouch."

"Sorry."

Tess smiled, grateful for the chance to regain her equilibrium. What on earth was he doing here? It was like her fantasy. One of her fantasies, at least. Where he came to her door, shaken and miserable, and begged her to be his, only his, for the rest of his life.

"I was just out this way," he said. "Shopping. Thought I'd drop by for a bit. I've got something I have to do in about an hour, so this is good. Thanks for letting me intrude."

Damn. So it wasn't that fantasy. Still, it was good, right? Or maybe not. Wouldn't this just encourage her to concoct more and wilder fantasies? Hadn't she just finished bemoaning her fate to her online buddies?

They hit the street, but Dash still kept his arm around her waist. The contact wasn't much, but it was very, very good. Despite her vivid imagination, she'd steeled herself to a future with no Dash. This was better. Oh, yeah. Although, she truly had no clue as to what it meant.

"So, uh, how was your interview with *Vanity Fair?*"

Dash hugged her a little tighter. "Same old. Although I liked the reporter. She was honest, and she didn't try and trick me. I appreciated her attitude."

"Was it a profile piece? Or something more specific?"

"It was about my father's retirement. Rumors are spreading. As far as I know, he's not going anywhere, but hell, who knows? When he does, that'll leave me in charge."

"Big responsibility."

He nodded, and when she looked at him, she was surprised to see his lips tight, his brow furrowed. Trouble in River City? "You don't want the job?"

He looked at her so sharply, she might have slapped him. She stopped, right where she was, causing a man behind her to curse at her. Not that she cared.

"You don't, do you?"

"That's ridiculous."

"Oh. Sorry."

"No, no. I'm sorry. I didn't mean to snap at you. It's…hard to explain."

"You don't have to." She caught his gaze and held it for a long moment. "But if you need to talk, I'm here."

"Thanks."

"Hey, you guys. Are we going to coffee, or what?"

She smiled at Mary's indignant stance, hands on slender hips, lower lip thrust out, right brow raised. "Yeah, yeah, we're coming. Jeez. Like you have so many things to do with these five seconds."

"Five seconds can be the end of the world," Mary said. "Or the beginning."

Tess thought about it, and Mary was right. All the big things in her life could be boiled down to around five seconds. When she decided to move to New York. When she understood that Brad wasn't Mr. Right. When she said yes to Dash Black. Five seconds.

While her head was busy with the notion, they made their way down the crowded street, past her favorite little bookstore, the Kosher butcher shop, the pizza joint that would have been great if she hadn't known the personal hygiene habits of the owner, and then finally to the coffee shop. It wasn't Starbucks, but it was close enough. Big chairs, nice patio seating, baked goodies, world beat music, and nice big cups of really hot, excellent coffee.

Dash went to the counter, and turned to them to get their orders. Tess liked hazelnut coffee, but Mary liked exotic concoctions that sounded more like ice cream sundaes than beverages.

Dash ordered black coffee for himself, and Tess got a kick out of watching the girl behind the counter. She'd recognized Dash, but she was trying to be cool. Her hands shook too much to pull that off, though. Poor kid. Tess knew just how she felt. Being around Dash was terrifying. In a good way, of course.

She wouldn't press him about the job thing. It was personal, and they weren't good enough friends—

They weren't even friends. Or lovers. Or anything, except employer and employee. At least, that's what she'd thought about fifteen minutes ago.

He'd been very clear about their situation, and

made no bones about the fact that they couldn't date. So what was this?

"Tess?"

"Hmm?"

Dash nodded toward the cup on the bar. "Your coffee."

"Oh. Sorry. Lost in thought."

"What about?" Dash walked with her over to the counter where they had the cream and stuff. She got one packet of sweetener and poured it in her cup.

"I was just wondering," she said, "if you came by today for sex."

12

IT WAS A DAMN GOOD THING he hadn't been drinking, or he'd have spit all over the floor. "Excuse me?"

"It's okay if you did. I mean, I'm not sure I would have said yes, but maybe I would have. I'm just curious."

"No, I didn't come by for sex."

Her lovely mouth curved down at the corners.

"Wrong answer?"

"Not at all. As long as you tell me the real reason."

"Fair enough." He headed toward the patio where Mary had secured them a table. He wasn't sure he wanted to go into this in front of Tess's friend. "Hold on," he said, then backed her up against the wall so they were out of earshot of any customers. "The truth is, I don't know why I came by."

"Oh."

"I shouldn't have. But then, I was thinking about you, and well, I was in the area…"

"You come out here often, do you?"

He smiled, knowing he was busted. "No. I never come out here. I was in the area because you're in the area."

That mouth of hers gave him a dazzling grin. "But, it had nothing to do with sex."

"I didn't say that."

"True, you didn't. But I'm still not clear about what it is you want."

He shook his head. "Sorry, can't help you. But as soon as I figure it out, I'll let you know."

"Gee, thanks."

"Look, if you don't want me to come by again, I can completely understand."

"You can come by."

"Even though nothing substantive has changed?"

"Substantive, huh?"

"I mean—"

"I know what it means, Dash. And I know what you mean. And I still say you can come by. I do, however, retain the right to change my mind."

"Fair enough."

"At a moment's notice."

"Absolutely."

She touched his wrist with her fingers. "Just be nice, okay? That's all I ask."

God, he wanted to kiss her. Right now, right here. But how could he, after she'd just asked him to be nice? Shit. He didn't feel the least bit nice.

"Dash?"

"What?"

"We'd better sit down before Mary does something I'll regret."

"Right."

She stepped away from the wall, and as she did, he stopped her with his free hand on her shoulder. Then he kissed her. Hard. He tasted her lips, and when she let him, he dipped inside to tangle with her tongue. When she touched him back, he nearly spilled his coffee. This was why he came by. And why he shouldn't come by again.

She deserved nice. Not him.

From: Erin
To: Tess

Re: Bonehead stuff

Wait just a fackin' minute here Ms. Big Dope Bonehead. Before we get to Mr. Unattainable and his, uh, rhododendron, I want to hear more about The Bitch. What did she do to you and where can I find her in order to make her pay. I happen to know a very Scary Guy who means business.

Seriously, Tess. Has this Lacey screwed things up for you? You know I'll help you out, don't you? I mean, I married Sebastian for his own rhododendron but the man also came with a serious bank account. (This is what happens when you're NYT fodder!) Please don't give up on the business. I know this is what you want. The Piggly Wiggly will always be there. And, dearie, I really don't think you're ready to retire to Tulip and give up on the paparazzi yet, are you? Promise me you'll come to me even if I'm a last resort. (And when you call, I'm going to scream this into your ear so it will be a permanent echo you cannot ignore!)

Now…Mrs. Dash Black? And why not? Don't you think he's tired of the fake and phony? And you, being real and honest and with no agenda…don't you think you look real good to him? (Obviously so, since he showed you his, uh, pool.) He'd be crazy not to be thinking about it even if he says nothing can happen between you two.

Seriously? Be yourself. So what if you don't know squat about inner peace and serenity.

I need to think about this and I'll definitely have my entire spiel ready when you call. You have been warned! Oh, Tess? One time when I was bemoaning what to do about Sebastian? You told me to do the opposite of what you would do. Well, turnabout time. All those women who fawn over him, treating him like God's gift to the women of planet earth? Yep. You do the opposite. Be your cool and rational and, okay, ditzy self. That way, whatever does or doesn't happen, you'll never have regrets, ya know?

Love you! Erin

Tess reread the e-mail, then turned away from her computer, her gaze settling on her wall hanging…Pin The Ear On Van Gogh. She'd gotten that as a little gift from Miss Mary last year, only she couldn't seem to find the ear. She felt sure it would turn up somewhere.

So Erin thought she had a shot with Dash. Hmm. Not the response she'd have figured. Erin was pretty levelheaded, and had been, even through the whole beginning of her relationship to Sebastian. Not that Erin hadn't taken major risks. If she hadn't, she wouldn't be married now.

God, if only Erin and Samantha lived closer. But Erin lived in Texas and Sam in Chicago, and the three of them had never met in real time.

The day Tess had gotten a computer, she'd found

Eve's Apple writing group, and she'd signed on in a hot second. Intelligent, creative women from all walks of life gathering together for an online book club...a delightful situation even if she hadn't been lucky enough to hook up with Erin and Samantha. Of course, the group at large didn't know about their Men To Do pact. That was private.

Just because Erin had married her Man To Do didn't mean Tess would. Yesterday, she would have laughed at Erin's notion that Dash was thinking about her as a potential...whatever. But since his surprise visit this afternoon, it didn't seem quite so ludicrous.

He'd come by to see her. Out of the blue. Oddly, she believed him when he said he hadn't come for sex. She also believed him when he said he had no idea what was going on. That, actually, was comforting. At least she wasn't alone in her befuddlement.

She turned back to the computer, and pulled up Samantha's e-mail.

To: Tess
From: Samantha
Re: Are you kidding

Wow, Tess! So shall we look for you on the cover of the *National Enquirer?* Just tell me they didn't take pictures of you while you were Doing It.

First Important Point: You're not a bonehead for sleeping with him! For heaven's sake, this is your Man To Do! Isn't that what this whole thing is about? Screwing men it's a bad idea to screw? Or did I get it wrong?

Of course I'm one to talk, I'm still wanting to snarl and hiss at everything with a penis. But once in a while I get the tiniest glimmer of my old urges so I know the Lust Thing will return and I'll outdo both of you. However! Mark my words. My Man To Do will remain just that. You two are giving women a bad name with all this I-slept-with-him-now-I'm-in-love stuff. Women can and do have no-strings sex and when it's my turn, I will prove it.

Second Important Point: Thinking about him all the time is totally understandable! The part that made me nearly choke on my extremely healthy snack of Oreos dipped in peanut butter was the Mrs. Dash Black part. Eek! Where did that come from?

And Now, The Extremely Important Conclusion: My advice? Squelch the Mrs. fantasies and relax. Enjoy the affaire for what it is. And when it ends, cry for a while, then carry the memories around and brag like hell to whoever will listen.

You know we will!

P.S. I was so into the sex, I forgot about the evil! What does this Lacey woman have against you? Don't tell me she's one of Dash's exes who sniffed out his attraction for you... Or is that too movie-plot?

Any strings you can pull, favors you can call in? Anything Dash can do? Or rely on your own charm, brains, strength and integrity. I'd like to think that can sometimes win out.

Failing that, a gentle shove down the stairs works wonders.

Samantha
Going back to her cookies

Leave it to Sam to tell it like it is. While Erin was wonderful and supportive, and her advice had merit,

Samantha's was a little closer to reality. Of course, given Samantha's recent history, it made sense that her head wasn't in the clouds. Poor kid had been devastated after her divorce from Brendan. She hadn't been able to find a Man To Do...in fact, she was having difficulty finding a Man She Didn't Want To Kill. But, given time, even Samantha would once again be up for a little slap and tickle. Maybe even her own...whatever.

Tess couldn't exactly call what was happening between her and Dash an affair. It wasn't even an assignation. Or a tryst. It was...something else.

Very possibly, it was nothing. At least nothing to get worked up over. Hell, the whole reason she was obsessed was undoubtedly because of who Dash was. She wasn't keen on the notion that she was starstruck, but what else was she to believe? One close encounter does not make for love. Sam was right. She should just chalk it up to an interesting life moment and move the hell on. She had a church to find. A class to enroll in. She had a business plan to attend to.

Bless Erin's heart for offering to help with the business. But Tess didn't want to turn to her friends. Of course, if things led to things, she would. Maybe. But not until she'd covered all her bases.

Which meant calling Cullen in the morning. No, wait, she had to do the Noir building in the morning. She'd call Cullen after.

Would Dash be there? She'd only seen him in the building a few times, and it was going on eight months since she'd gotten the job. She did see Patrick most every time, though.

There was an interesting guy. Something told her there was more to him than met the eye. The way he took care of himself, the almost paternal role he'd taken with reference to Dash. She'd considered asking Patrick out, but figured mixing work and play wasn't a good idea. Ha. Her night with Dash sent that theory to hell and back.

Maybe she should talk to Patrick about the situation. He was approachable, and more than anyone else, he wouldn't be put off by Dash's celebrity.

Tess sighed. Stood up. Walked over to the counter and poured herself another cup of green tea. No way was she going to talk to Patrick. Was she nuts?

Yes, of course she was.

Mary was convinced that Dash was looking for a safe, no-strings attached, open-door invitation to her bedroom, which Tess should put a stop to immediately, if not sooner.

Samantha thought she should go for it, and take no prisoners.

Erin voted for the possibility that this could be the start of something big…and permanent.

Tess was clueless. Which wasn't an unnatural state for her. But jeez, this was a rather big honkin' deal. She was the one who had to live with herself. Who would face the consequences if she fell flat on her face.

One thing she'd learned in her dealings with Men Who Want Sex But Not Commitment…every time she hooked up with one of them, they'd told her exactly who they were and what they wanted right off the bat. Gary, back in Tulip, had told her on their first

date that he was going to go to California and become
a movie star. No mention was made of taking a wife
with him. But what had she done? Figured he'd
change his mind.

Wrong.

Frank, the only other guy in Tulip she'd liked, had
told her he wasn't looking for anything, you know,
serious. Had she believed him? Not even close. The
more they dated, the surer she became that he'd get
serious. Real serious. And, she supposed, he had. But
not with her. He'd started dating Shirley Slattery
about two weeks after he'd broken up with her. Married Shirley three months after that.

Which led to her first New York boyfriend. Cole
Darden. Gorgeous Cole. With his six-pack abs, his
chiseled jaw. His startling blue eyes. His first date
message? He didn't believe in love. Said it, just like
that. "I don't believe in love." Tess had laughed.
Told him he'd change his tune when the right woman
came his way. Subtext? Wait'll you get a load of me,
baby. Outcome? Dumped, like yesterday's trash, after
she'd made the fatal mistake of telling him she had
"feelings" for him.

After Cole came the ever popular Brad. She
couldn't even bear to think of the mistakes she'd
made with him. Starting with thinking he'd ever want
a woman like her.

God, but she'd been naive. The guy had won the
birth lottery by being drop-dead gorgeous and richer
than sin. When he'd come on to her at that party,
she'd nearly fainted. Lord, he'd been smooth. But not
as smooth as Dash.

Good grief, what her life had become. She felt like she'd woken up in *Dynasty*, only without the wardrobe.

Tess took a sip of tea, and realized she'd let it grow cold. She put the cup in the microwave, then did some calf stretches while she waited for the ding.

Once armed with steaming tea, she went over to the couch and curled her legs underneath her. A few sips, and she felt a bit better. Physically, at least.

Emotionally, she was so low she could roll with the dust bunnies. What had Dash made perfectly, unmistakably clear? He was not, repeat not interested in a relationship. He was not even interested in a second date. He'd taken her to the party as a favor. He'd slept with her as a perk.

"So, Ms. Wizard," she said aloud. "What can we conclude from this walk down memory lane? That I'm an idiot."

Oh, man. She was. A royal blue idiot. Completely delusional. Dash Black and her? Please. It was ludicrous.

She put her cup down, and spread herself out on the sofa. Flopping one arm over her eyes, she took a couple of deep cleansing breaths. Then she made up her mind. She'd forget about Dash. She wouldn't torture herself with fairy-tale endings. She wouldn't even play the "what-if" game.

And she'd go back to Plan A. Find a man who was the opposite of Dash in every conceivable way, and marry him.

DASH TOOK ANOTHER BITE of the seared Ahi, enjoying the rich texture and taste. Which was about all he was enjoying. Whoever invented award shows should be shot.

Okay, so maybe there could be the Academy Awards. The Tonys. The Grammys. The Emmys were okay, too. But that's it. None of the others. It had gotten right out of hand. Most had more to do with publicity than excellence.

But then, wasn't that the game? Wasn't everything he did, everything everyone he knew did, all about the publicity? Publicity meant revenue. And revenue was king.

So here he sat, along with all the other schmucks with a company to promote, a name to get in the trades, at yet another post-awards banquet. Trying not to drink too much. Forcing himself to smile.

And he wasn't even with someone he liked.

Kate was beautiful. Kate earned about twelve million dollars per picture. Gross, not net, but hey, it was still a damn hefty sum. Kate had a body that made millions of young men across the world stay too long in the john.

Kate was also about as stupid as a human could be, and still hold a job.

She giggled at something someone said, then leaned over to whisper in his ear. She had a thing for whispering.

"Dash, I have to go tinkle."

He managed to stifle his cough. Smiling brightly, he turned to whisper back. "Do you need some money?"

She blinked a few times, then shook her head.

"Do you need me to walk you there?"

"That would be great."

"I'd be delighted." He folded his napkin and put it next to his plate. Then he took hold of his wineglass, and drained the sucker. Fortified, he stood, and offered Kate his hand.

Flashbulbs went off in two directions. He barely acknowledged them. This was the job. This was the life. This was...

Shit. He wished Tess was here.

Kate stayed close to him, but blessedly silent, except for the kissy noises she made to every guy they passed, all the way to the rest room. Once she disappeared into no-man's land, he relaxed, leaning against the wall in the darkest spot he could find, and his thoughts went right back to Tess.

He still couldn't figure that one out. Going over to her place yesterday had been, well, nuts. What had he thought was going to happen? Sex? Okay, sure. Sex. But then again, that wasn't why he'd gone. Not really. He'd thought about her a lot. The odd thing was, what got to him most, what really stuck, was her laughter after she'd realized she'd lost most of her fake nails.

He couldn't think of one woman he'd been with, ever, who would have reacted in just that way. The women he knew, even the terrific ones, took their looks damn seriously. They had to, given what their world was like.

But even those women who weren't in the public eye, at least the one's he'd dated, would have been mortified to find themselves in Tess's situation. Some would have laughed it off, sure, but that would have been a cover. Not something genuine.

Tess had laughed like it was the funniest damn thing she'd ever done. It didn't ruin her night. Not in the least. She'd just cracked up at her own foolishness, then moved on.

Was that, shit, he didn't even know what to call it, joie de vive, what he had gone after? Was that what had drawn him back to her?

In a word, yes.

He'd had fun with her. He admired her. He'd dreamed about her lips, her curves. She was bright. Funny. She could dance. All bonuses, right? Sure. Except what was he going to do with her?

Take tonight. He'd had this on his schedule for over six months. His publicist and Kate's had worked out all the details. They were a good match. She was going to make an appearance at the gala, which would help him raise money for cancer and AIDS research. He was a hell of a lot more marketable than her real boyfriend, a young man from Idaho who wanted to become a prize fighter, and probably could have if it wasn't for his penchant for getting knocked out in the first round of every fight.

Now, if he dated Tess, what would he do about nights like this? Hell, most of his nights were exactly this. Different celebrity, different award or fund-raiser or what have you, but the same. Business. That made it to the front pages of the tabloids.

What woman would put up with that? He couldn't stop seeing other women. It wasn't possible. The whole Noir empire was built on the idea of the single life. He represented the fantasies of over a million readers who wanted to live vicariously through his exploits. While he figured most of them would like Tess, it wasn't really what they were after.

They wanted the Kates of the world. The Renes. The Julias. They wanted the glamour and the glitz, and they wanted to believe he scored with every one of those lovely creatures. Of course, if he had, he would have been in the *Guinness Book of World Records,* but that wasn't the point, either. This was about fantasy, not reality. And the cost of his membership was that he remain the player. Maintain the illusion.

Which meant a normal relationship with someone great like Tess was out of the question.

On the other hand, Tess was a reasonable, down-to-earth kind of gal. Someone who could laugh at herself, and keep her dignity. If he explained the situation, maybe she'd understand. Maybe she'd have no problem with him keeping up appearances.

"Wow, you've never smiled at me like that before, Dash."

He jumped as he looked directly into Kate's eyes. He hadn't even seen her. "You look beautiful," he said, years of practice paving the way for the perfect comeback. When all else fails, flattery works every time.

"Oh, that's so sweet!" She leaned over and kissed him, lingering so the photographers would have plenty of time to get all the shots they needed. Finally, she stepped back. Smiled. "Let's go back to the table. I want to see who gets best actor. I hope it's not Kevin. He's so nasty. I don't like him."

"I'm sure he's heartbroken about that."

She shook her head, her sparkling hair shimmering

in the lights. "I don't think so. He probably doesn't even know."

"Well, for his sake, I hope he doesn't find out."

She took his hand in hers. "That's what I like about you, Dash. You're such a gentleman."

"You flatter me."

"No, I mean it. You're about the nicest great looking guy I know. You don't ever say mean things."

"I'm not that nice, Kate. Trust me."

"Oh, pooh. I know what I know. And I'm not as dumb as everyone thinks."

"No one thinks you're dumb."

They reached the table, but before he could pull out her seat, she turned to him. "See? I told you. You would never do anything to hurt anyone."

"I would, Kate. And I have. I'm no saint."

"Yeah, but you wouldn't do it intentionally."

He got her seated, then settled in beside her. His wineglass had been refilled, for which he was grateful. Kate might not be the brightest bulb in the chandelier, but her words had certainly given him pause.

Even if Tess agreed to see him on his terms, was that smart? Wasn't it likely she'd end up hurt?

Naw. Not Tess. She was too levelheaded to get romance and sex mixed up. She'd say yes. She would. And it would be fantastic.

Nothing wrong with sex for sex's sake. Hell, the whole Noir legacy was built on the idea. So why not go for it?

13

TESS HAD JUST FINISHED her e-mail and shut down
the computer. She was in her old bathrobe, the che-
nille blue that always made her think of home. She'd
scrubbed her face, and even given herself a little fa-
cial, and her bathtub was full, waiting for her to sink
her bad self down to soak. Tonight's aromatherapy
was lilac, with bath salts, after-bath moisturizer and
even a spray-on cologne. On the little desk by her
bed, she'd prepared all the fixins for a pedicure,
choosing Corvette red as the color du jour. All was
right with the world, if one ignored the persistent,
nagging Dash thoughts that continued to plague her.

She'd gone to Noir this morning, but Dash hadn't
been there. He had, it seemed, made the papers the
night before, however. After he'd left the coffee shop,
he'd gone to the Golden Globes with Kate Whistler.
Tess had always hated her movies. The ditz.

But, what did Tess expect? That he'd go out with
her once, renounce his former life, eschewing all starlets as so much nonsense, and beg her to be his, only
his?

Right. That was gonna happen.

She shook her head, mystified as usual by her own
mind. Where was her logic, her reason? The common

sense God gave a goat? She needed to stop thinking about him, for heaven's sake.

Right. Like that was gonna happen, either.

She put on music, Debussy, and adjusted the volume to perfection. Then she went into the bathroom, the sight of her claw-foot tub, the best thing about her apartment, in fact, the only good thing about her apartment, and slipped off her robe.

Just as she put her right foot in, the doorbell rang. She cursed, wondering if she should bother. If it was Mary, she could call later. If it wasn't... It had to be. No one else came over.

The bell sounded once more, and she donned her robe again. She'd tell Mary to get lost, then continue with her spa treatment. Nothing felt better than pampering herself, except being pampered by someone else. She flashed on Dash, and for a silly moment, thought it might be him at the door. Yeah, right.

After unlocking the dead bolt, she swung the door open. "Mary, I'm just about to get into the bathtub—" It wasn't Mary.

"I should have called," Dash said. "I wouldn't want to keep you from your bathtub."

"It's you."

"Yes, it is. But I also have wine." He held up a bottle, which Tess didn't look at. She was too busy being mortified by her Ma Kettle bathrobe.

The bottle came down to his side, and his smile faded. "Look, I'm sorry. I had no business dropping by like this. I'll give you a call tomorrow."

He turned, but Tess caught his hand. "No, it's okay. You just surprised me. Come on in."

"What about your tub?"

She grinned. "It can wait. Why don't you find the bottle opener in that top drawer." She nodded to the kitchen. "I'll uh, be right back."

"You're not going to change, are you?"

"I'd thought about it."

"Don't. I think you look great."

She coughed out a burst of laughter. "Well, we both know what you're here for." Then she winced, wishing she could take it back. Jeez, what a maroon. She was about as subtle as a Mac truck.

He blushed. She watched it happen. Dash Black's cheeks got pink, as did his neck. Wow.

"Actually, I came to talk to you."

"About?"

"I think I'd like to open the wine first. In fact, I think I'd like to finish at least one glass before I begin."

She went to the cupboard and pulled out two cut crystal wineglasses she'd inherited from her Aunt Pearl. "Pour away."

He found the opener on the first try, and removed the cork with the grace of a sommelier. Before she could truly start to panic, he poured them each a glass.

"To...possibilities," he said, holding his up.

"All rightie then," she said, finishing the toast with a clink of crystal. She took a sip. Her tongue did the happy dance, which led to the second and third sips. "My God, this is fabulous."

"It's from our private reserve."

She blinked at him.

"Don't look at me that way."

"I'm not looking at you any way. Except curiously. Shall we go into the drawing room?"

"After you."

She led him the few steps to the couch, then she curled up in the corner. She wrapped her robe around her legs and tightened her belt. It was weird, being naked underneath the robe. Not that he hadn't seen her naked, but still. It felt awkward.

She wanted to push him into talking, but held back. He sat in the middle of the couch, sinking down far too low. Damn couch. Older than mud.

He turned to look at her, smiled, then leaned forward to brace his elbows on his knees. He held his glass with both hands. "I had this planned out, but now…"

Shit. This didn't sound good. Her heart sank like a lead balloon as she watched him struggle to find the words. "Are you trying to tell me I'm fired?"

He jerked back on the couch. "No."

"That Cullen turned me down?"

He shook his head. "No. Nothing like that."

"Well, Pat, I'd like to buy a vowel."

"Huh?"

"Never mind. Just spit it out."

"Okay," he said, more to himself than her. "Here's the thing."

She leaned forward waiting. "Yes?"

"It's like this…"

Where was her wine? Evidently, this was going to be a long evening.

"My life is a little…peculiar."

"Uh-huh."

"I mean, it's not like I have a nine-to-five, where I go to work at the same time every day, come home the same time."

"I kinda figured."

He eyed her for a quick second, then resumed studying his glass. "Part of my job is, uh, escorting certain ladies to certain functions."

"Yes, I know. We talked about it."

"Right."

"And?"

"Oh. But see, even though I go out with these ladies, I'm not actually dating any of them."

Her tummy tightened. "Okay."

"Despite what you read in the papers. I mean, my God, they have me shacked up with every actress from Sandy Bullock to Kirstin Dunst. But, well, here's where it gets tricky. The stuff they write about me? I don't discourage it, exactly."

"You don't?"

He shook his head. "You know that old saying, 'Any publicity is good publicity?' That's been true as far as Noir goes. It happened this way to my father, too. It's the nature of the beast."

"I understand." She nodded, sort of, maybe seeing where this was heading. Or not.

"So, while my social life is really busy, my personal life…isn't. Which is okay. I'm not complaining. I know I've got it made and all that. But there's something missing."

"A documentary crew to follow you around?"

He sat back, looking at her crossly. "I'm being serious here, Tess."

"Oh. Sorry."

He raked a hand through his hair. "It's okay. You can say whatever you want."

"Go on. I won't be a smart-ass again. At least for the duration of this conversation."

He nodded. "Okay, where was I?"

"Something was missing."

"Right." He took a big swig of wine, swallowed, then coughed for several seconds. When he'd gained his equilibrium, he scooted closer to her. "I had a good time the other night."

"Me, too."

"A really good time. And I'm not just talking about that thing at the pool."

Her heart beat so hard in her chest, she wondered if she was going to die, right here, in her non-Victoria's Secret robe. All wisecracks fled from her overexcited brain, and she forced herself to breathe.

"I don't want it to end there. I'd like to see you again."

"You would?"

He nodded slowly, meeting her gaze with his own. He wasn't kidding. Not if his expression was to be believed.

Oh, God.

"But, you would still…"

He nodded. "I know. It's a lot to ask. It's not fair, and I have a hell of a nerve even asking."

"Well." She tried to think. Of anything. Except that Dash Black was asking her to be his… "So, what, exactly would I be?"

He winced. "Uh… Friend with benefits?"

Oh. Not exactly the fairy-tale ending she'd hoped for. At least he was being honest. Brad hadn't done that. He'd led her to believe they had a future. With Dash, she knew exactly what she was getting. The

most interesting, incredible man she'd ever met
wanted her...on his terms.

It was everything she didn't want offered by the
man she wanted more than anything. God had a
wicked sense of humor.

She felt a hand on her leg, and realized she'd been
staring for a long moment. "I'm, uh, processing."

"You don't have to make a decision right now.
And believe me, if you decide you'd like to at least
try this, it's not going to be solely about me. I won't
have the kind of time I'd like to spend with you, but
I'll do everything in my power to make you happy. I
know you have a business to run, and I won't interfere."

He met her gaze, and studied her as if seeing her
for the first time. "I want to look forward to you. I
want to know you're there, even when I'm on the
road. I want to talk to you on the phone. I want to
wake up and see you in my bed. You're the most
fascinating woman I've met in a long time, and I want
to learn everything about you."

"I...I don't know what to say."

He moved closer, leaning in. "Then don't say anything." His lips touched hers in the gentlest of kisses.

Her eyes fluttered shut as she abandoned the tur-
moil of her mind for the sensual delight of his mouth.
His tongue ran over the crease of her lips, then slipped
inside. She uncurled her legs to get nearer to him, to
let his arm go around her back and pull her close.

The kiss deepened, and memories of their night together kicked off a chain reaction in her body. A
moan escaped before she realized it, and she found
herself returning the kiss with passion, parting her lips

under Dash's. This was too good; this was death by pleasure. How could she possibly say no to this on a semiregular basis?

The thought made her break the kiss. "Uh, Dash?"

He cleared his throat, tried to look as if he hadn't just had his tongue down her throat. "Yes?"

"Would we have to hide?"

He shook his head. "No. Not at all. I wouldn't do that. But you have to realize, I won't be able to take you to the big press events."

"But we can go to dinner. To a movie?"

He smiled, but it was kind of sad. "Yes. I'm not ashamed of this, Tess. Far from it. I think you're terrific, and I don't give a damn who knows it. But I do have to keep up the pretense. A lot of people count on me. I have more to consider than just my own feelings."

She hadn't really thought about that, but now that she did, the notion was rather startling. He was the symbol of the red-blooded American male, and all that represents. Noir employed thousands of people. It seemed hard to fathom that dating her could threaten that, but then she didn't know enough about it to make that call. What she did know was that her whole generation had been raised on Michael Black and his exploits. That Noir was a part of the fabric of their lives, and that it wouldn't have had nearly the impact if Michael had been married to a nice plant lady.

With Black senior getting on in years, Black junior had become the figurehead of Noir. Of course he couldn't just abandon his whole empire for the likes of her.

"Talk to me," he said, his voice gentle and coaxing.

"I don't pretend to understand your life," she said, "but I do see that you're in something of a predicament. So I'm not insulted or anything."

"But?"

"But I don't know if this is something I can deal with."

"I don't, either. That's why I want you to think about it for as long as it takes. I don't want either of us to get hurt."

"I vote for that."

He smiled again. Touched her cheek with the back of his hand. "I hope the answer is yes, but I'll understand a no."

She opened her mouth, but she couldn't think of what to say. He'd taken her by surprise, and a hundred thoughts tumbled in her head.

Dash took care of the problem neatly by standing up. So he would leave, and she would ponder. Good thing she didn't need any sleep or she'd be in trouble. Right. Then she looked up at him and saw a wicked gleam in his gaze, a hot promise. He held his hand out to her. "I believe I interrupted something."

She put her palm in his, and he pulled her to her feet straight into his arms.

"You're so beautiful," he whispered. "And I can't get you out of my mind."

"I think that was my line."

His brows arched. "Really?"

She nodded. "I don't know, Dash. I'm not sure I'm sophisticated enough for all this. I'm from Tulip,

Texas, for God's sake. The biggest event there was the annual Tulip festival and rodeo.''

''That's all this is, Tess. One big Tulip festival, with lots of bullshit thrown in for good measure.'' He kissed her chastely, then sought her gaze again. ''Think about it. Take as long as you need.'' Stepping back, he took her hand once more and led her through the kitchen toward her bedroom.

Only he made a slight detour to the bathroom. ''I wouldn't want you to skip your bath because of me,'' he said, his voice as steamy as the air in the small room.

She felt his hands on the collar of her robe, and she undid the belt as if they'd been planning this for days.

He kissed her neck as he stripped her bare, then, from behind as he continued to nibble and lick, he ran his hands over her chest, moving slowly, inching his way to cup her breasts.

It occurred to her that this time, she was the naked one, while he was dressed. And once again, they would be wet, and not just from excitement.

He rubbed the flat of his palms in slow circles, just brushing her hardened nipples. She shivered with the sensation. Dash stopped and walked over to the side of the tub. ''Get in.''

She obeyed in what felt like slow motion. The candles flickered in the steam-filled room, the scent of lilacs filling her with a calm that seemed impossible.

The water was still nice and warm, and he held her hand as she stepped in. She shivered again, a quick frisson that gave her goose bumps and harder nipples.

Bracing her hands on either side of the tub, she

sank into the perfumed water, moaning as she was cradled in warmth. Shutting her eyes, she leaned back and ran her hands over her slick stomach to her breasts.

His moan made her look, and she was grateful to see that he was taking off his shirt. It would be tight, but they could both fit, with a little maneuvering. Debussy still played, a musical web spun all around them.

She sighed again, waiting for Dash to finish undressing, staring at his incredible chest, then back to his face. He was achingly handsome. Far more gorgeous that she ever dreamed of being, and she knew that his looks were part of her desire to say yes. Was that wrong? Was it shallow to want him because he was beautiful? Because he was Dash? If he was a mechanic, would she ache like this?

God, she had no idea. How could she? Perhaps, in time, the shock of who he was would die down, and she'd see past his looks, his fame. But in order for that to happen, she needed to be with him, talk to him, get to know him as he claimed he wanted to know her.

What if she said yes, and then she found out later she'd been mistaken? That it was the hype that made her heart crash inside her chest, that turned her bones to jelly.

She could change her mind, that's what.

Because, what if it wasn't that at all? What if it was Dash, the man, the completeness of him, who she wanted so badly she could scream?

Dash moved, and she saw that he hadn't taken anything off but his shirt. He knelt by the side of the tub, reached over to her little shelf and got the sea sponge and the bath gel.

He grinned as he poured a liberal amount of the green goo into the sponge, then played with it until it was all suds.

"What are you doing?"

"Is there a name for a male geisha?"

"Jerry Lewis."

He laughed. "So quick," he said. "So wet." Then he squeezed some suds onto her chest, between her breasts. "I think this is going to take a while. So if you need more hot water, you just say so."

"No, no. I'm fine. I'm…"

He smiled at her as he moved the sponge to her body and began a long, slow, circular caress. "What?"

"I forget."

"Good. Now close your eyes and let me do all the work."

"This is terribly decadent. Hedonistic. And if you stop, I'll kill you."

He chuckled just as her eyes closed. Lilacs, "Claire de Lune," as the sponge moved down her belly. It was a dream, something so lovely she couldn't have imagined it on her own. She felt special, beautiful and more desirable than any woman on earth.

Which was an illusion. She wasn't, and she'd never be. She was still Tess Norton even if Dash Black wooed her. Tess Norton, who'd made every wrong decision a girl could make when it came to men. Who'd sworn to her dearest friends that the next man she went out with would be the marrying kind. The ordinary kind. The boring kind.

The sponge moved down to the juncture of her thighs, and then the sponge disappeared and it was his hands, his fingers, that touched her just so…

She'd think later.

14

DASH WATCHED HER FACE AS his finger played along her nether lips. With her eyes closed, her face flushed and relaxed and her short hair spiking wildly, she looked like sensuality itself. He drank her in like wine, his need to please her as acute as the stiffening in his slacks.

He dipped inside her and her mouth opened in a perfect O. She inhaled deeply holding the breath as he slowly rubbed her clit.

"You like that?" he asked.

She nodded.

He leaned closer to her ear. "Talk to me."

"Oh, my."

He couldn't help but grin. "Tell me what you like. What you need."

"Deeper," she said, her voice soft and thick.

He obeyed, and she arched in the tub, her breasts coming out of the water wet, hard tipped, lush. "What do you want?" he asked again.

"More."

Instantly obeying, he slipped two fingers into her, remembering to thrust deeply.

The rosy flush spread across her neck and face making her impossibly more beautiful. He wanted to be in the tub with her—

"You," she said.

"What do you mean?"

"I want you. Need you. In here with me."

The plan had been to make her come. To give her such pleasure she couldn't say no to his proposition. But the more he pleased her, the stronger his own desire became. That's not how it usually worked for him. Not that he didn't enjoy lavishing attention on his partners, but this was different. He *needed* her to come.

"Dash."

"Yes?"

She turned to him and half opened her eyes. "You asked me what I wanted."

"You're right." He left the pleasure of her heat to stand up and take off the rest of his clothes. Her gaze went straight to his cock, and that O came back to her lips. He couldn't resist. The way she lay in the tub, the angle, those lips. He moved closer, and her hand went to the base of his shaft with wicked confidence. When she lapped the head, he groaned, his whole body getting tense and tight.

She held him steady, and he heard the water splash a bit, but couldn't look to see what she was doing. He didn't want this over in two seconds, so he fisted his hands, gritted his teeth, but she wasn't making it easy.

Her tongue circled and teased as her hand moved slowly up and down. Dammit, he wanted to thrust but he held back. He felt as flushed and full and ready as he'd ever been in his life; and not just in his cock, either—the entire length of his body, the backs of his eyelids, his earlobes, the backs of his knees, the strip

of aching flesh between balls and anus—every plea-
sure-laden part of him was suffused with sensation,
pulsing, linked by a million sizzling nerves to the
wanton, erratic movement of Tess's mouth.

He gasped when he felt her palm, filled with warm
water, cup his balls. It felt amazingly good. Too good.
With more strength than he thought he had in him,
he pulled back. He wouldn't come yet, and if he let
her continue, it would be inevitable. No, he wanted
to be inside her.

She pouted prettily, but he'd change that in a moment. Grabbing the big lavender towel off the bar
behind him, he spread it open between his hands.
"Come," he whispered.

She braced her arms on the tub, then stood, rising
like Venus, and he drank in the sight of her dripping
and shiny. God dammit, she turned him on.

Carefully, she stepped onto the braided rug by her
feet, then stepped into his arms so he could wrap the
towel around her. Taking advantage of the situation,
he kissed her as he rubbed her back, wanting her naked, needing her dry.

Well, not in some places.

He smiled, breaking the kiss, which wasn't so bad
because it meant he could concentrate more on her
dryness, and less on his erection. In fact, while rubbing her down in a way he hoped was soothing and
sensuous, he surreptitiously checked out the bathroom.

Bigger than it should have been for the apartment,
it had the typical commode and standing sink. The
tub was the true centerpiece, and Tess had decorated
around it. Nothing fancy, just candles and plants, one

picture on the far wall of a reclining nude that he liked a lot.

Which brought him right back to Tess. Actually, as he was drying the luscious orbs of her ass, thinking about anything else was completely out of the question.

He slowed down, using his index finger to pull the towel between her cheeks. She gasped as he ran the towel up and down the slender crevice and he didn't stop until he felt her shiver.

"Dash?"

"Hmm?"

"You're a kinky bastard, aren't you?"

"I do my best."

"Really?"

He nodded, liking the feel of her soft hair against his cheek. "Curiosity may have killed the cat, but it does wonders for the pussy."

She bit him on the shoulder.

"Ouch. What'd you do that for?"

She looked up at him, a wicked grin making her perfect. "Because I could."

"Ah. Another highly desirable trait."

"What?"

"Seizing the moment."

Her hand, through the towel, grasped his still hard cock. "Like this?"

"Ah, yeah. I think you're dry, what do you think?"

"Actually, you missed a spot."

He met her smoky gaze. "Uh-oh. Where would that be?"

She let him go, then slipped out of his embrace. "Come with me and I'll show you."

He was right on her heels as they entered her bedroom. He liked it immediately. The king-sized bed helped, with its fluffy white comforter and pillows. The fact that it was also a four-poster gave him all sorts of ideas.

With her typical abandon, she sprawled across the comforter, her head cradled by her plethora of pillows, her arms spread wide, and her legs curled enticingly. He joined her, running his hand over her tummy and breast and he nestled next to her.

She moved in to kiss him, but instead took his lower lip between her teeth and nibbled.

He retaliated by taking her right nipple between his thumb and finger.

She nipped.

He squeezed.

She moaned.

He let go, deciding on a better tactic. He brushed the skin down her torso, her tummy, and found exactly where she was still wet. His fingers, already familiar with the terrain, zeroed in for maximum reaction. Which he got. In a move destined to haunt his nights, she arched her body, opening her mouth as she moaned, letting go of his lip.

Not one to ignore an advantage, he kissed her, hard, thrusting his tongue between her lips, tasting her, taking her, as his fingers drove her wild.

It simply was too much, and he had to be inside her. He pulled back from the kiss, gasping for air. ''Condom,'' he said.

She nodded, then turned her head to the small nightstand beside the bed. Hating to move from her heat, he scrambled as quickly as he could to open the drawer. The box of Trojans was right there, and in what must have been land record speed, got one out, opened, and on his cock. A moment later, the hell with the drawer, he spread her legs so he could kneel between them.

The sight was too tempting for slow seduction, and he was too hungry. He ran his hands up her thighs, and when he got to her soft patch of hair, he petted her for a moment, then his thumbs found her lips, which he spread apart. He leaned down, drunk on her scent, and tasted her.

She moaned as her hand corded through his hair.

With single-minded intensity, he applied the hardened tip of his tongue to the swollen nub, and he didn't stop when her legs wrapped around his back, or when she bucked beneath him so hard he almost lost his balance. He didn't stop until her whole body tensed into a single purpose, and when she cried out, when she came with a violent shudder, he surged forward to bury himself to the root inside her.

She clutched him, still spasming, with her interior muscles in what had to be the most incredible sensation on earth. He pulled back, almost all the way out, then slammed into her again, rocking the whole damn bed.

Her hands went to his back, her nails digging into him, and her legs squeezed his back. Tess keened her pleasure, formless words, sounds from somewhere deep in her chest, her head thrashing on the pillows, her face flushed and shiny with a sheen of sweat.

He wasn't going to last like this, but he didn't care. He couldn't be in her deeply enough. Again and again he thrust, her contractions milking him to the point of no return. The pressure increased as his balls tightened, and in a single moment outside of time, he came, and came, his voice the roar of a lion, the victory of the beast.

He held still, the pulsing from her and now from him an incredibly intimate dance. Breath came to him in great gulps, and he struggled to focus his gaze.

What he saw when he did kicked up his determination about ten notches. Tess, her beautiful face in repose, her eyes closed, her lips moist, her satisfaction evident in her liquid grace.

She smiled, still with closed eyes. "Golly."

He laughed. "Golly, indeed."

She gave him another squeeze with those amazing inside muscles, and his whole body shuddered. "Imagine what it would be like if we practiced."

"My point, exactly."

She opened her eyes, at least half-way. "You don't play fair."

"Nope."

"What if *I* want to see *you?*"

"I'll do whatever I can to make sure I can comply."

"But if you have to date Nicole Kidman, I'm out of luck?"

He grimaced. "Sometimes, yes. Maybe it would help to think of me as a doctor. Called out to see patients. It would be hard, but understandable, right?"

"As long as you're not giving mouth-to-mouth."

With great regret, he moved, taking care of the condom first, then curling up next to Tess so he could touch her. "I won't do that. If you ever see anything like that, a kiss or a hug or anything that bothers you, please remember that what you see isn't always what's real. Photos can be manipulated. I've been the victim of that many times, and frankly, it sucks.''

She sighed. Turned her head slightly to the left. ''Before I say yes or no, I want to know what it's like to wake up to you.''

''Then I'll stay.''

She closed her eyes again. ''Good.''

THREE-TWELVE, AND SHE WAS wide-awake. Dash lay beside her, his hip against hers, the only point at which they touched. But she heard him breathe, and the sheets felt different, and if she moved, she might wake him.

Her body, pleasantly sore from that amazing lovemaking earlier, really wanted to shift. Actually, to get up, stretch, wash. So why not just do that? It was her bed, after all. He was a guest. A lover.

Her lover.

If she wanted him to be.

How could she say yes to him if she couldn't even get out of bed? How could they be equals if he was Dash Black and she was just Tess?

It made no sense for her to agree to his plan. She'd end up losing. Big time. Crushed, flat, like a bug under a shoe. She'd undoubtedly fall in love...hell, she was halfway there already, and then? Long lonely nights wishing he was with her? Jealousy every time she saw the *National Enquirer?*

No. Not a good idea. A stupid idea, in fact.

However...

She tossed the damn comforter aside and got out of bed. Dash didn't move a muscle. See? All that worry, and for what? She scolded herself as she padded to the bathroom.

After taking care of the necessities, she put her whitening toothpaste on her brush and started in on her molars, staring at her reflection.

Her hair looked as though she'd stuck her finger in a socket. The raccoon look was also quite disturbing, damn her makeup remover. Ah, and the pièce de résistance, she had the beginning of a zit on her chin.

What in hell did Dash see in her? She wasn't buttugly or anything, but gee whiz. She was an ordinary woman. Special, sure, but not the cover of *People* special.

She spit into the sink, then rinsed and used the Scope, careful not to gargle too loudly. One more searching look at herself. A close-up, then back farther.

She wasn't bad, despite those pesky ten pounds. In another world, a normal world like Tulip, Texas, she'd have felt good at this weight. In fact, most of what was troubling had to do with not being in a normal world. Lacey had her there. It was true, Tess didn't belong, and would never belong. Brad was a stretch, and Brad was no Dash.

''Well, shit.''

What if Samantha had it right? Play while the playing is available, because it wouldn't be forever. The whole reason Tess had left Tulip was because she'd promised herself she wouldn't let fear stop her from achieving her goals. At the end, she wanted to look back at her life and have no regrets. Certainly none from being a chicken.

The one thing that was certain about Dash was that

he was not going to fall in love with her. Not going to marry her. This was about sex. Fun and sex. Sex and more sex. Which was by no means a bad thing. As long as she didn't confuse it with love.

And there, as they say, was the crux of the matter. Okay, so she had two cruxes. But if she said yes to the sex part, and truly understood that it wasn't about more, then the not belonging part was no big deal, right? She belonged in her bed, and boy did Dash belong in her. Good golly Miss Molly, but he was incredible. She got all squirmy just thinking about it.

"So," she said to the woman in the mirror, "to do Dash or not to do Dash?" She laughed, turned off the light and headed back to bed.

Dash was still sleeping. Which made sense, given the hour. She should leave him alone. Poor guy must be worn out after what they'd done. On the other hand...

She coughed. Again. No luck. At least she could stare all she wanted, although the light was too dim for really excellent checking out. But even in the dark, he was the most beautiful man. With that sculpted chin, strong nose, eyes that made grown women weep. All in her bed. Damn.

Her hand went to the light on her nightstand before she could stop it.

He winced.

She sat down, a little harder than was necessary, then coughed again.

Bingo.

"Hey," he said, his voice all growly from sleep. "What time is it?"

"An ungodly hour. Go back to sleep."

His hand went to her thigh. "Come here."

"Okay." She laid down and scooched up next to him. "Are you in any way coherent?"

"Depends. If you want to talk philosophy, no. If you want me to lick something, you bet."

She smiled. "No, I want you to hear something."

"I'm all ears."

"Yes."

He cleared his throat. Blinked up at her a few times. "Yes?"

She nodded as she ran her foot up his calf. "Yes."

His eyes widened. "Oh. Yes."

"Uh-huh."

"This is good. This is very, very good."

"I know."

"You're sure?"

"Yep. But I reserve the right to change my mind."

"Of course. Wouldn't have it any other way."

"But this doesn't change anything about Cullen. I'm still doing this on my own."

He yawned, then pulled her closer to his body. "I'm always glad to help, but I won't interfere."

Something kinda hard poked her hip. "Uh-oh. I think I woke everything up."

His chuckle made her shiver, but not as much as the feel of his lips on the curve of her neck.

She reached down between them to find his almost-there erection and give it a helping hand. Turns out, it needed no help at all. Despite the hour, Dash Junior was as eager as a pup for morning walkies.

She pushed Dash onto his back, which made him grunt in surprise, but she didn't care. Then she pushed the comforter all the way off the bed as she got another condom from the drawer. She'd have to get more. Lots more.

Once the packet was in hand, she turned her attention to Dash. She straddled him, almost sitting on his thighs. A quick minute later, Junior had on his rubber, which didn't seem to bother him in the least.

She laughed as she adjusted herself so she was right over her target.

Dash held himself steady so that she could watch him as she lowered herself inch by slow inch, filling herself with him. "Oh, goodness, you're a big boy," she said.

Dash groaned as his hips lifted. "And yet I fit so well."

"That you do." She was down all the way and she sat for a moment relishing the power of her position, the future of their affair. "I think, Mr. Black, that I'm going to use and abuse you, if you don't mind. Try everything I've ever wanted. No holding back. I'm going to be brave and brazen and I'm going to wear you out."

He groaned again. His hands went to her hips, held her steady, and thrust so hard she was lifted off the bed.

"I'll take that to mean you approve."

"Tess?"

"Yeah?"

"You can do anything you want to me, any time you want, however hard you want. But right now, if you don't lift that beautiful ass of yours, I'm going to have to get rough."

She grinned. "Cool."

15

DASH EYED HIS SCHEDULE with distaste. Meetings, interviews, editorial decisions, lunch with Guiliani, drinks with the attorney right after, then dinner with the editor of *Vanity Fair* at an AmFar fund-raiser.

What he wanted to do was go back to bed with Tess.

He couldn't stop thinking about her. Last night, hell this morning, was unbelievable. He hadn't felt this energized in a long time. Problem was, he'd have to really restructure his life if he wanted to spend time with her.

Kelly came in with a latte, and she looked at him crookedly.

"What? Spinach in my teeth?"

She shook her head. She'd been with him for over two years, and they knew each other fairly well. She was in her mid-thirties and her husband worked for Noir as a graphic artist. They had a great son, Jason, who was eight. Kelly tended to treat Dash with that same mothering instinct she used on Jason. No one got past her who shouldn't. She made sure he ate well, that he wasn't too booked up, that he didn't let social amenities fall by the wayside. All in all, an excellent assistant. "Something's different," she said.

"Can't think what."

"It's not your hair. Or the clothes. It's something…I don't know. But I'm right."

"Kelly, you're always right. However, there's nothing new about me."

"Yeah, there is. And I'll figure it out, too. Just you watch."

"Hey, not to change the subject, but this AmFar thing tonight, how important is it?"

"Pretty important." She went over to the wing chair across from his desk and sat down. Kelly was a little pudgy, which he rather liked. She looked soft and warm. Pretty with a minimum of fuss. She wore her Wisconsin farm heritage proudly. "The Clintons will be there. And a lot of heavy hitters from the business who should be coming to the gala."

"Damn."

"Why, you have a hot date?"

He shot her a look.

She grinned broadly. "So that's it."

"What?"

"Someone has breached the castle. Who is it? Nicole? Sandy?"

"Neither. I mean no, I don't have anyone in my castle. Whatever the hell that means."

"You lie like a rug. That blush is a dead giveaway. Come on, Dash, tell me."

"Nothing to tell."

She raised both brows. Which meant he was busted. "All right, I am seeing someone. But it's nothing serious."

"Who is she?"

"Her name is Tess Norton."

Kelly's mouth opened then closed. "Tess of the plants?"

He nodded.

"Tess that I know? From Texas? With that incredible smile?"

"That would be the one."

"Oh, my heavens. Dash Black, you devil. This is wonderful."

"Wait a minute. It's not wonderful. It's not serious. It's just…you know, for fun."

"Fun my big fanny. This is a real woman, Dash. Not one of those conceited movie stars you hang around with. She's bright and ambitious. And she makes the best corn bread I've ever tasted."

"She cooked for you?"

"Oh, she just brings in treats now and then. She gave Patrick a scrumptious lemon pound cake for Christmas."

"Really."

"Yeah. She's like that. Nice." Kelly frowned and looked at his inbox.

"What?"

"Dash, you know I think you're the greatest. I love working for you, and I try never to stick my nose where it doesn't belong."

He barked out a laugh, which was quieted by a sharp stare.

"But I'm not sure about this. Tess is…"

"What?"

"She's not exactly naive. But she's also not a real player."

"What, and you are?"

"No. But that's not the point. I'm not dating you."

"I still don't see the problem."

"You're a pretty easy guy to love."

"Why, Kelly. Does Paul know you feel this way?"

"Don't get cute. Listen to me. Be careful. She can break."

He nodded, all joking forgotten. "I'm being as honest and straightforward as I can. I've told her there are certain places I can't go."

"Lots of places."

"She knows. And she still wants to try."

"Okay. I'll keep my fingers crossed."

"Won't it be difficult to type?"

"Oh, I'm gonna—"

"Yeah, yeah. So you say. But you never."

"There's always a first time."

He grinned. "So are we sure I can't back out of AmFar?"

"No. You can't. And Patrick wants to see you."

He nodded. "I'll go after I make a call."

She got up, straightened some papers on his desk, then smiled at him. "For what it's worth, I think you have great taste."

"Sure. I hired you, didn't I?"

"Oh, man. And here I forgot my hip boots."

"Go away, Kelly."

"Yes, sir. Right away, sir."

He waited till she was past his door to pick up the phone. He dialed Tess's cell phone, but her voice mail came on. When the beep sounded, he almost hung up. Then an idea struck him. "Hi, Tess. It's me. I'm not a hundred percent sure on this, as I might have to go to a benefit, but are you free tonight? Call me." He hung up, his thoughts racing, wondering. He was pretty sure he could talk Patrick into taking his place, but then what? What would the press think? The world at large didn't know Patrick existed. They didn't associate him with *Noir*, and he certainly hadn't been fodder for the gossip mills.

On the other hand, it was just one night. One night Dash could be spending in bed with Tess.

He would talk to Patrick. Now.

To: Erin, Samantha
From: Tess
Subject: The Cliff From Which I Jumped

Hey Gals,
This is what he said, verbatim: "I'd like to see you again." This is what I said (kind of): "Okay."
There was some more conversation, yada, yada, yada with the end result being he spent the night, and we agreed to see each other even though he still has to date Nicole Kidman, which isn't as bad as it sounds because it's his job, and he has all these people working for him, so he can't let them down.
So, how about those Mets?
Oh, and please tell me I'm not certifiable.

Love and kisses
Tess

To: Tess
From: Erin

No, doofus. You are not certifiable. (Dash might be…Nicole Kidman? Puh-lease!) You are a woman on a mission. You have a Man To Do.

So, he's THE playboy of the western world. Who cares? You're the one who matters! Are you really "okay" with "seeing him again"? Whatever happens, I just don't want you to get hurt. You told me once to indulge in Starbucks and chocolate and I think the same can be said here. Breathe deeply. Remain calm and focused—which means enjoy the sex. And do not fall into any sort of groupie trap. You deserve better than just crumbs from his table. You deserve to be the centerpiece!!!

Love you! Erin

To: Tess
From: Samantha
Re: Cliffs and other stuff

Tess! I am sorta getting excited here (no, not THAT way). Dash wants to see you again. Wow. Sounds like a pretty long-term commitment for that guy! Maybe you'll have Erin's luck and he'll fall for you. (Stop laughing, oh she-with-less-than-respectable-self-esteem, it's perfectly possible. Nicole Kidman is undoubtedly dull company next to you.)

Of course you realize that you have a chance to live every woman's fantasy here. To be the one that can make a guy like that wake up and think, "Suddenly I know the meaning of life—to be Tess's love slave for all eternity."

Okay, I know I'm getting ahead of myself. Perhaps even being a tad romantic. Nice to know I'm still capable of it!

I had my own disaster last night. Met a guy in a bar, thought I was ready for a Man To Do adventure, thought he was a good one. Two kisses and all this negative emotion starts pouring out of me. I cried all over his fancy suit, can you believe this? I was so embarrassed. Of course he freaked completely. So I guess I have to wait awhile longer until I try again. Too much emotion still too close to the surface. But I'm definitely in recovery.

So Tess, from my new less-cynical position, I would say you should keep hope to a safe minimum, but enjoy every minute. Sometimes you just gotta say, "what the f*ck" and risk the heartache in order to live.

Keep us posted! And if it turns out he's a playboy to the core after all, then we're here to cry to for the time it takes you to get over him and move on.

Samantha

DASH SHIFTED HIS BAG TO his other hand, then knocked, looking back to make sure he'd picked up the right bulbs for the hallway. Damn super. Damn building. He hated coming all the way here to see Tess. If she'd been a different woman, he'd have put her up in an apartment near his place. But if she had been a different woman, he wouldn't be in this situation to begin with.

It still shocked him that he felt so strongly about her in such a short time. Sure, he'd liked what he'd seen all those months she'd done his plants, but after that one night...

Why? He hadn't a clue. And who cared? She'd said yes, and he was determined to make her happy about the decision. He said a silent thank-you to Patrick. Tonight he would be the official representative of Noir at the benefit. He'd seemed happy to do it, actually a little excited. Which was great. Better than great. Not that Dash would take advantage of him, but in a pinch.

And speaking of pinches... He knocked again, and jumped back when the door flew open. Her smile, wide and excited, made his heart slam in his chest.

"I'm so glad it's you," she said, as she tugged him inside.

"Who else would it be?"

"I don't know. Mary. The mailman. Santa. But it's not. It's you."

He laughed, put down the bag and scooped her into his arms. "And it's you. Isn't that a lovely coincidence?"

She hugged him tight around his neck, her shining eyes were close enough for him to see the gold specks among the green. But then her eyes closed, and her lips touched his.

Her kiss lit him up like a Christmas tree. It was more than just taste or texture or any of the physical stuff. It was electricity and tension and it went to his head and his cock at the same time. He wanted her, but like no one he'd wanted before. And he'd been with some incredible women. But Tess, ah, God, she was...different.

He let it all go, and pressed against her, letting her feel what she'd done to him. From zero to upright in thirty seconds. Maybe there was some kind of record book he should call.

"Mmm, you taste like cinnamon," she whispered, her lips still touching his.

"You like that?"

She nodded.

"I'll make a note of it."

"Please do. And while you're at it, I should tell you a few other things I like."

"Shoot."

Her hands moved down his back until they were splayed squarely on his ass. "Great buns. Don't know what you do to keep them like this, but don't stop."

"Work on buns. Check."

Her hands moved again, up his sides then onto his chest. "Same goes for the chest." She kissed him, then pulled back just enough to talk. Just enough for her breath to mingle with his. "And the wearing of silk is also approved of."

"Chest, check. Silk, got it."

"I guess that's it," she said.

He frowned. "Really? That's all you like about me?"

"I think your name is sexy."

"Thank my father, not me."

"I will, the moment I meet him."

"And?"

"And, what?"

"You weren't going to, uh, continue?"

"Oh. Yeah. Well, there is something else I'm pretty sure I like. Although I probably need to do some more hands-on exploration. Just to make sure."

"And what would this something be?"

Her hands moved slowly down his chest to his waist. She lingered there, making him crazy, rocking back and forth slightly, as if she heard a song meant only for the two of them. He nudged her a bit, his impatience more to do with the strain against his zipper than his lack of enjoyment of the moment. He liked her playfulness more than he could say.

She moved down a little farther, until she touched his hipbones. Then she stopped.

Dash groaned, nipped at her nose. "You probably can't tell," he said, "but one of us is pretty excited here."

She rubbed against him, adding to his torment. "Which one?"

"You," he said.

"That's true. But am I the only one?"

"I don't know. You tell me."

Her hands moved down until she cupped his erection. He hissed with the feel of her, even through the material.

She giggled. Not one of those high-pitched nasty giggles, but a deep, throaty giggle filled with promise. "All indications seem to point at you being moderately excited."

"Moderately?"

"Yeah. I think you're just getting started."

"Oh, baby…"

"But I just remembered."

"What?"

She squeezed him. "The other thing I like."

"Oh?"

"Yeah." She rose on tiptoes and brought her lips to his ear. "Your taste in clothes."

"Hey!"

She leaned back and laughed at her colossal joke, and all Dash could do was shake his head. "You're a nut."

"I know."

"A beautiful nut."

She stilled. "You think?"

"I know."

She inhaled deeply and let the air out in one slow, smooth breath. "So far, I'm liking this arrangement."

"So far, me, too."

"Except for one thing."

"What's that?"

She gave him a wicked grin. "We're wearing entirely too many clothes."

"Oh, that."

"Yeah," she whispered, squeezing his now completely hard cock once more. "That."

He took hold of his shirt, raw silk, hand made in Hong Kong, and ripped it open, sending buttons flying across the room.

She gasped and brought her hands to her mouth.

He ripped one of the wrist cuffs in his mad panic to get naked, and when he was finally free of the shirt, he pounded his fists on his chest and gave his best impression of the Tarzan yell.

Which evidently wasn't very good, as Tess burst out laughing so hard she doubled over, clutching her stomach.

Not exactly what he'd had in mind.

There was only one thing to do. He'd distract her.
He had ways.

"DASH? YOU AWAKE?"

"Yep."

"That was fun."

"Yep."

"Who are you trying to be, Gary Cooper?"

"Nope. Trying to sleep. It's after two."

"That's not my fault. You're the one who wanted
thirds."

"I know. But now it's time to sleep."

"DASH?"

"Hmm."

"You asleep?"

"Yes."

"Really?"

"No. Not anymore."

"Oh."

"What?"

"I was just thinking."

"What about?"

"Ice cream."

"*What?*"

"Rocky road."

"You're serious, aren't you?"

"Yeah. But I'll live without it."

"Are you sure?"

"Yeah."

"TESS."

"Wha…"

"Wake up."

"What time is it?"

"Three-thirty. Come on. Get up."

"What's going on?"

"Here."

"Huh?"

"Rocky road."

"Rocky... I don't have any... You went out?"

"Yeah."

"For me?"

"Yeah."

"Oh, my."

"You did say rocky road, right?"

"Uh-huh."

"So what's wrong?"

"Nothing. Everything's...perfect."

"Jeez. Women. I'll never understand them."

"I don't know. It seems as though you understand me pretty darn well."

"Hey, I thought you wanted that ice cream."

"I do. And I'll eat it. After."

"After? Oh."

"Yeah. Oh."

16

"PATRICK? YOU HAVE A minute?"

He looked up from his computer and smiled. "For you, Tess? Of course."

She walked farther into his office, wondering if she'd lost her mind completely. Patrick, although nice as could be, was completely dedicated to Noir and was arguably the backbone of the whole company. He made tough decisions, watched the bottom line and he wasn't in the habit of doing any of the spokesman work. Until lately, that is. So not only did she want to ask his advice about maneuvering Dash away from his work, she also wanted to push Patrick into disrupting his orderly life to take over the movie-star-dating portion of Dash's life. Right. "Whatever it is can't be that bad," he said, turning to face her as she sank down into the overstuffed chair across from his desk.

"I wouldn't be so sure," she said.

"You're not quitting, are you?"

"No. Although you may want me to after this conversation."

His smile waned and she was mildly surprised at how attractive he was. Not close to Dash's stunner class, but really handsome, much more so than she'd thought before. What was it? New glasses. Yes. And he was leaner. Tanner. My goodness, Patrick was re-building himself, and doing a damn fine job of it. Perhaps his move into the spotlight wasn't the negative she assumed.

"I'm not much of a mind reader, Tess, so..."

"Sorry. Okay. This isn't easy, so bear with me."

"I'm all ears."

"Well, uh, first, I guess you know I'm sort of see-ing Dash."

Patrick nodded. "I'd heard."

"He told me, right from the get-go that he wasn't, you know, available or anything."

"I see."

"Because of Noir, of course. I mean, even if he hadn't told me I'd have assumed he didn't want a commitment."

"Why not?"

She stopped, her mouth open, her speech, im-promptu but not too lame, lurching to a dead stop. "Are you kidding?"

"No. Why would you think he wouldn't be inter-ested in a commitment?"

"Because he's Dash Black."

"And that means what?"

"Come on, Patrick. You know this better than I do. His job. Jeez, he dates a different movie star every week. He's the world's most eligible bachelor. He's the epitome of sex without strings."

"Ah."

She eyed him more carefully, looking for a twitch or a hint of a smile. "You're making fun of me, aren't you?"

"Not at all. In fact, I've been thinking about you and Dash a lot lately."

"Why? Cause I'm screwing everything up?"

"No. Because I haven't seen him this happy in years."

Her heart slammed in her chest and she held back a gasp through sheer will. "Please don't screw with me about this, Patrick. It would be very mean."

"I'm not. I'm completely serious. At first, I didn't think it was a very good idea, him going out with you, but now I'm rethinking my position."

"You are?"

"He'll never admit it, Tess, but Dash doesn't care much for the spotlight."

"Come on."

"I'm not joking. He does it effortlessly, so it appears that he's in his element, but he'd be a hell of a lot happier if he could sit by the sidelines and out of the public eye."

"So why doesn't he quit?"

Patrick's brow rose just enough for her to get the silliness of her statement.

"Right. But that leads us back to what I was saying. It's not possible for anything to, you know, happen between us. Nothing long-term, I mean."

"If you know that, then what's the dilemma?"

At the cold truth of his words, Tess shrank back against the overstuffed chair. "Oh, hell. I don't know. There shouldn't be one. I know what I know, and I can't do a thing about it."

"But?"

"I guess I was hoping for a loophole."

Patrick smiled, his face taking on a hint more Dash

with the tilt of his lips and the shape of his even, white teeth. "Tess, the whole world is made up of loopholes. Things change in a heartbeat."

"True. But I want them changed my way."

"Ah," he said, his voice amused, but not making fun. "There's the catch. If you know how to make that happen, let me know, okay?"

She nodded. "Any, uh, hints? Tips? Advice?"

He leaned back, tapping the edge of a pencil on the arm of his black leather chair. It was an odd rhythm, but familiar somehow. She didn't say a word while he tapped and stared somewhere past her right ear. She did, however, have time to plan many exciting ways that she could get creamed by Dash...would get creamed. Doomed. Jeez.

"Do you have a stereo system?"

She jumped at Patrick's voice, shifted back to the conversation instead of her tiny, vivid picture of the hell her life was going to become. "Yes."

"Do you have any classical CDs?"

She nodded. "A couple."

"Who?"

She had to think a minute. "Vivaldi. Debussy. Tchaikovsky. Why?"

He pushed back in his chair then stood, and she noticed immediately that he'd lost weight. Since she'd known him, he had something of a beer belly. Not anymore.

"While you're doing whatever you're doing, could you please tell me how come you look like a *GQ* model?"

He laughed. "No wonder I like you, Tess. You've got a way with words."

"Come on. You look fabulous."

He stood next to her, touched her shoulder and gave it a gentle squeeze. "Thanks. I've made a few changes in my life, including diet and exercise."

"Bravo. Anything special?"

"Nope. Just the stuff I've always known I should do."

"Damn, you don't have any magic answers, do you? What good are you?"

"Not much," he said, grinning. "Hold tight."

She did as she watched him open up a cupboard by his bookshelf. Rows and rows of CDs were all lined up in a disgustingly orderly fashion. Tess couldn't see what he was pulling out, so she waited patiently. Well, almost patiently. By the time he'd chosen a dozen, she was on her feet. With two floors left to go, she still had a few hours of work ahead of her, and she hoped, hoped, hoped Dash was going to come by tonight.

Patrick turned around. "Take these. He likes them all. A lot. Not that music is going to change everything, but it's the only way he can totally relax."

Her own brow rose. "You sure about that?"

He shook his head. "Good luck, Tess. I hope for your sake and his it all works out. But don't be too disappointed if it doesn't. He's been groomed from birth to take over this company. Sort of like Prince Charles with less money and better perks. He won't find it easy to disappoint Dad."

"I know. I'll be the most surprised kid on the block if we last a couple of months."

"So enjoy what you have right now."

"I will." She lifted her armful of CDs. "Thanks."

"It's not much. If I think of anything else, I'll let you know."

She leaned over and kissed his cheek. "Thanks, Patrick."

"Any time."

DASH CALLED IN SICK. Technically, he should have called in tired, but that wouldn't cut it. He'd spoken to Kelly, who'd given him the gist of the day, and what he could do from home. Of course, he wasn't home. He was still with Tess, had been since nine the night before, and now it was almost eleven IN THE MORNING, and they hadn't left the bed, except when absolutely necessary.

Damn, what a time they'd had. Perfection. Right down to the music. It was uncanny how her taste mirrored his own. All the way down to Eric Satie. He'd never expected this from a girl from Tulip. Actually, he'd never expected it from anyone. This was a whole new ball game.

Tess smiled up at him, and if he'd had an ounce of energy left in him, he felt quite sure he'd be hard again. Made him wonder how he'd managed to get it up so many times in the last fourteen hours.

She was unbelievable. So hot he should wear asbestos. Even her laugh turned him on. He felt like a kid. Dopey with lust and raging hormones.

"I'm hungry," she said.

"Again?"

"I ate dinner last night at six. I don't think it's unreasonable for me to want breakfast."

"Granted. So, what do you want?"

"Deli."

"Does that mean you want to venture out?"

"Yes. Because I have no deli on the premises."

"Hmm. That means getting showered. Dressed."

She wiggled her brows. "I'll wash your back if you wash mine."

"What about the front?"

"We can do that too."

He grinned, threw back the covers, and rolled out of bed. He stretched, feeling muscles he wasn't used to feeling. He'd have to change his workout if this was going to become a regular thing.

Huh. Who was he kidding? It was already a regular thing, and he had no immediate plans to change that. He liked being with Tess. She made him happy, and not just when he was with her. Of course, the downside was that when he went on his work outings, he had a bit of difficulty concentrating on the woman he was with. And he'd coerced Patrick into stepping up to the plate a few times too many. But screw it. He liked her. A lot. More than he should, given the circumstances. But that was probably the newness of it all. They'd only been together four weeks. Things would cool. Things always cooled. He turned back to the beauty on the bed. "Come on, lazybones. You're the one who wants bagels."

She groaned as she got up, and he just looked at her while she mimicked his stretches. He even recognized her grimaces. "Sore?"

"Oh, yeah."

He kissed the tip of her nose. "Sorry."

"You should be. Jeez. What do you think I am? An acrobat?"

"Excuse me? I was there. I know exactly who did what to whom."

"Oh, yeah. Well, then fine. Let's go shower. And brush our teeth."

"Great idea."

"I'm chock full of them."

He walked to her side, and ran his hand over her silky back. "I know."

She sighed, leaning in to him. "There is a very real danger that if you start touching me, we may not get out of here for a while."

"And that would be bad, how?"

"When I expire from hunger, you're going to have a lot of explaining to do."

"Point well taken." He grabbed her hand and they entered the spacious bathroom. She went to the tub, drew the shower curtain around it, and started the water while he dug into his overnight kit for his toothbrush and paste. By the time she stood next to him at the sink, he was minty fresh.

She followed suit while he climbed under the hot water. It felt like heaven on his weary bones. Closing his eyes, he let the shower work its magic. He opened them again when Tess joined him.

He abandoned his perfect position so that she could get wet, grabbed the soap and lathered his hands really well. Then he went to work making sure Tess was squeaky clean from top to toe.

Breakfast turned to lunch, and by the time they got to the deli, they were both ravenous. Unfortunately, their lunch wasn't the quiet idyll they'd hoped for. The couple in the booth next to their's got a bit overexcited about Dash's presence, and had to have autographs and pictures taken. In the midst of ordering their meal, a gaggle of tourists jostled around the table, shoving envelopes, menus, in one case the back of a hand, for his signature. Two people asked Tess for her autograph, and while she tried to explain that she wasn't a celebrity, they would hear none of it. She signed as her cheeks heated in embarrassment.

"Sorry about that," Dash said, when they were finally alone.

"About what?"

"You having to put up with all the celebrity crap."

"I'm okay. I don't mind."

"This wasn't bad. It can get very bad."

"How so?"

"Interrupted meals. Rudeness. Touching. The touching is the worst."

"I won't have to worry about that, though, right?"

"If you're with me, I would count on it. I've seen it happen time and again. Most folks are nice. Polite. Some folks are downright jackasses."

"Okay, you handle the jackasses, and I'll take care of the nice and polite."

"Got it. Good plan."

She grinned. "You know what?"

"Hmm?"

"I like you."

His head tilted slightly left as his gaze softened. "That seems convenient, given that I like you, too."

"You're not who I expected you to be."

"No?"

She shook her head. "I thought you'd be an arrogant bastard."

He laughed. "I am an arrogant bastard."

"No, you're not. Not even close. And believe me, I have a Ph.D. in such things. You're a nice guy, which is surprising given your background."

"It may appear that my youth was filled with ribaldry and hedonism, and I suppose in some ways that's true. But generally, I was just a kid. School, baseball, smoking in the bathrooms, that kind of thing."

"You never talk about your mother."

"I didn't know her very well. She and my father were only together for a year. She decided she'd be happier in Europe, where she was born. She died when I was five."

"I'm so sorry."

He shrugged. "As I said, I barely knew her."

"Still, growing up without a mother is tough."

"I had nannies, housekeepers. They kept me on the straight and narrow. And Dad was a pretty tough taskmaster. If I didn't have the grades, I was in for it."

"Sounds like my dad."

"What does he do?"

"He's the manager of a big hardware store in Tulip. He loves to build things. You should see his woodshop. It's amazing."

"And your mother?"

"She's a professional gossip. She lives for the dirt. Although, I will say that she's a very nice gossip. She loves to hear it all, but then she constructs alibis for everyone's dark deeds. Honestly, she should be a writer. Although how interesting would it be if there were no bad guys?"

"You love them a lot."

"That I do."

"Sisters? Brothers?"

"Nope. Just me. But lots of cousins. Lots and lots."

"I just have Patrick."

She smiled. "He's terrific."

"Yeah."

"What do you think of the change in him?"

"What do you mean?"

She blinked. "In Patrick. You know. The hair, the body."

Dash shook his head. "I'm not following you."

"Wow. Next time you see him, *see* him. You'll be surprised."

"Okay, I will."

The waitress arrived with their food, and Tess chowed down on her bagel and scrambled eggs, just happy to be where she was and who she was. She almost forgot about everyone staring. Almost.

DASH STOOD AT THE DOOR to the gym, studying Patrick as his brother jogged on the treadmill. Patrick looked fit, as fit as Dash had ever seen him, but Tess had been right. Something more had changed. Dash shifted into work mode and looked at his brother as if he were studying a cover layout.

Glasses. Patrick wasn't wearing any.

Hair. Darker, thicker. Interesting.

"Hey, stranger," Patrick said as his thick tennis shoes thudded on the belt. "Decided to come to work today, did we?"

Dash grinned. "Yeah, can't let you have all the fun."

"Some fun. I had to meet with Jefferson alone."

"Ouch. Man, I'm sorry. I forgot."

Patrick slowed his pace. "You've forgotten a lot in the last few weeks."

Dash walked over to the weight bench, put his gym bag on the floor and sat down. "Yeah. I guess so."

"It's Tess, isn't it?"

Dash nodded, and Patrick jumped off the treadmill. He wiped his brow with the towel he'd worn around his neck, then leaned against the front of the machine. "Talk to me, bro."

"I don't know what to say."

"You can start with what the hell you're thinking."

At Patrick's sarcastic tone, Dash frowned and shot him a glare. "That sure as hell makes me want to spill my guts."

Patrick sighed. "Sorry. It's just that I told you about Tess. She's a nice kid. A really nice kid. What's going to happen to her when you get tired of this little dalliance?"

"It's not a little dalliance."

"No? So you're saying you want to stay with Tess? Live with her? Marry her?"

"Come on, Pat. You know better than that."

"I do, but you don't seem to. I don't mind stepping in to cover for you now and again. In fact, I've been rather enjoying myself. But buddy, you have some heavy responsibilities, not the least of which is to make sure you don't break this girl's heart."

Dash looked up at the ceiling, staring at nothing, thinking of this morning as he pulled Tess into his arms. He couldn't imagine not feeling her again. Not tasting her.

"Dash?"

He focused again. "Yeah."

"Are you in love with her?"

"No. I don't think so. I like her a hell of a lot. I think about her too damn much. Shit, Patrick, I don't know anymore. If things were different..."

"There's something you should know."

Dash quirked his brows.

"Dad's going to announce his retirement at the gala."

All the air seemed to leave Dash's lungs in one great sigh. Like a prince hearing his king was on his deathbed, the weight of Dash's responsibilities came crashing all around him. Once his father stepped down, there was no turning back. He would be Noir. Sure, at some point in his life, when he was in his fifties perhaps, he could reasonably find someone to settle down with. But not now. Not in the near future. It would change things too much. Be too risky.

So where did that leave him? Could he possibly continue to see Tess? Talk about living in a fishbowl. He couldn't put her through that.

He felt Patrick's hand on his shoulder, giving him an encouraging squeeze. "You have some decisions to make. I hope you consider all your options."

"All my options? What options?"

Patrick looked at his watch. "Shit, I have to get out of here. One of us has to run the damn company. But I will say this. You do have options. Think them through. Remember, nothing changes if nothing changes. I'll talk to you later."

"Hey—"

"Later," Patrick said as he headed toward the

locker room. "Oh, I've got a new restaurant for you to try when you're in L.A."

"L.A.?"

Patrick stopped. Even from this distance, Dash could see him roll his eyes. "The Golden Globes. This weekend."

"Oh, shit."

"Jeez, Dash. Get it together, man. You can't afford to fall apart now."

Dash stared at his hands. He was falling apart. Tess. He shouldn't be with her at all. But how could he let her go?

THE MUSIC FELT evocatively familiar. Nothing she could put her finger on, no single composer came to mind. But the melody struck something old inside her. Something that lifted her melancholy mood.

Tess put down the bag of potting soil and headed toward the sound. There were no plants to tend at this end of the penthouse, and she'd never gone this far. Dash was home, she knew that, and evidently listening to a wonderful stereo.

The closer she got to the music, the more connected she felt to it. She'd find out what it was and buy the CD as soon as possible. Figures Dash would have exquisite taste.

The hallway walls had a beautiful Asian pattern of bamboo and leaves, with the thick, beige carpet below and perfect recessed lighting. The entire apartment was fabulous, but this was the first place she'd felt he lived in. The door on her right opened to his bedroom, and she couldn't resist a peek inside. The huge bed was the centerpiece, and the great armoire and chest of drawers fit Dash. Sturdy, simple, clean lines.

He had books in built-in shelves, and a nice sized television, complete with sound system and DVD. The bed itself looked inviting with a fluffy green comforter.

She debated exploring further, but the music called, so she left his room and continued down the hall. She passed a bathroom bigger than her living room, and finally came to a door at the end of the hall. Slightly ajar, she could hear the eloquence of the single piano.

Knocking lightly, she pushed the door open, and found Dash wasn't listening to a stereo at all. He was at the keyboard, his body swaying as he played.

She'd had no idea. He'd never said a word about this, not once. Which seemed odd, as the music was clearly a big part of his life. No one played that well without hours and hours of practice.

Her gaze moved to his fingers, and as they tripped along the keys, she felt a shiver remembering how they had felt running over the inside of her thigh, the curve of her neck. He'd hummed at times, pretty snippets of melody that he'd tossed off as tunes he'd heard but couldn't identify.

The piece built toward its crescendo, his back muscles tensing beneath his Oxford shirt as he poured himself into the music.

She held her breath as he played the final notes, and the echo of the final chord hung in the air like perfume.

"So you've found out my secret," Dash said. He turned around then, his expression unreadable.

"I'm sorry. I shouldn't have come back here. The music was so beautiful—"

He shook his head, stood. "It's okay. I should have invited you before now."

"You never even mentioned that you played."

"It's something I hold pretty close to the vest. A private passion, if you will."

"What was that piece?"

He shrugged. "Something I wrote a while ago."

Her eyes widened in surprise. "You wrote that? My God, it's gorgeous. Have you recorded it?"

He walked to her side, kissed the words away. "No, I haven't recorded it. It's a hobby, that's all. Nothing for the masses."

"I guess I can understand, but it seems a shame. I'm no expert, but that was stunning."

"You're stunning."

She smiled as she looked into his eyes. "I could use a hug."

"My pleasure," he said, wrapping her up in his arms.

She held on tight, needing his strength. Breathing deeply as her eyes fluttered closed.

"What's wrong?"

"Cullen turned me down."

His grip on her tightened. "I'll call him."

Her eyes flew open as she pulled out of his embrace. "Don't you dare."

"He hasn't thought this through, Tess. If he had, he'd have seen you're offering him a perfect investment opportunity. It's a misunderstanding, and I can fix that with one call."

"I appreciate it, Dash, but no. I told you before.

This is my baby, and I'm not going to have you running interference.''

He gave her a stern look, clearly not pleased with being shut out. ''I'm not offering this because we're sleeping together. Knowing the circumstances gives me a better perspective. If I didn't believe in your abilities, I wouldn't make the offer.''

Tess had been thinking about this very thing all morning. She'd debated even telling Dash about Cullen's call, but she'd dismissed the idea of hiding it. She wanted no lies between them. She'd struggled with the idea that Dash could help, could grease the wheels, but every time she'd convinced herself it would do no harm, she'd been filled with unease.

Perhaps Dash was right, and all he would accomplish would be to clean up the mess Lacey had made, Tess would still feel obligated. That was the crux of it. She was pretty damn clear about where this relationship was headed, and it wasn't a pretty picture. How could she make clear decisions about what to do if she felt obliged to him?

''Dash, I appreciate it. More than you can know, but I can't let you step in. This is mine.''

He shook his head, ran a hand through his hair. ''Okay, fine. But do me one favor. Don't let it end with Cullen. Go talk to him in person. The worst that can happen is he won't change his mind. But give him a chance to see who you are.''

''He said no. How can I possibly—''

''Trust me on this, okay? Just go. Try. If he says no you haven't lost a thing.''

The thought made her tense, and her immediate reaction was to refuse point-blank. But this was her future, and Dash was a very astute business man. If she couldn't take his help, she could at least take his advice. "All right. I'll talk to him."

"Great. I may be off base here, but I don't think so. You deserve this, Tess. Don't let Lacey have the last word."

At the mention of her name, Tess knew what she had to do. She'd see Cullen, but not until she'd paid a little social call on Lacey Talbot.

Dash leaned down and kissed her gently on the lips. "I wish we had more time. I came home to pack, and dawdled on the piano." He smiled sadly.

"Pack?"

He nodded. "I have to fly to L.A. for the weekend. But I'll be back Monday night."

It shouldn't have hurt to hear him say that, but it did. Big time. This sharing him with others was for the birds. But, she'd known what it was going to be like from the get-go. So she smiled, pretending it was just another day in paradise. "I'd better go see to your plants."

"I'm sorry."

"It's okay," she said, forcing brightness into the words. "Just don't have too much fun."

"Trust me, I won't."

She kissed him once more, then headed down the hallway. As she passed his bedroom, she wondered why he hadn't invited her to stay with him. Why it was always at her place.

Her heart sunk deeper with each step. She was his back-door girl, his bit on the side. Is that truly what she wanted? The crumbs instead of the cake?

The longer this—*thing*—went on, the harder it was going to be when it ended. And end it would. The only question was when.

17

DASH ADJUSTED HIS TIE AS the limo came to a halt at the Beverly Hilton. He smiled at Helen, his date for the evening. She was up for Best Actress, and he hoped she won. He liked Helen, liked her work, her sense of humor. They'd teamed up once before, when she'd just split from her husband, but there had been no romantic sparks. Just friends who understood the game.

The reporters were out in force, of course, with the NBC cameras taking center stage. But there was *Entertainment Tonight, E!, Comedy Central,* and a half dozen other large camera setups. Interspersed were the print journalists, the photographers, the sound people, security, and enough movie and television stars to give a groupie a heart attack.

It would take them an inordinate amount of time to make their way up the red carpet. The Beverly Hilton was well equipped to handle the crowds, even the bleachers set up a safe distance from the actual celebrities, but it was still a nightmare. The runway was warmer by at least ten degrees than the air outside the enclave of fame and fortune, and Dash thought that was probably a good thing for all the beautiful ladies in their revealing gowns.

Helen had her long, blond hair straight, almost to

her waist, covering a nude back that was quite fetching. Her gold gown hugged every curve, although, like so many of the women on display, he wished she'd put on a few pounds.

Smiling in that public way that was as automatic as breathing, he stopped for the first interview. *E!* They asked all the usual questions, made the same insinuations, trod no new ground at all. Dash didn't mind. He didn't want to be there. Didn't want to fully engage. He wanted to be with Tess. In her cozy little postage stamp of an apartment. With her head on his shoulder, watching reruns of *Friends*.

HER HEART NEARLY BEATING out of her chest, Tess rang the doorbell of the old brownstone, then tried to remember how to breathe. Maybe Lacey wasn't home. She probably wasn't. Tess hoped she wasn't.

What in hell was she going to say to the woman? Stop being mean or I'll tell on you? Why do you hate me? What would it take to make you go away forever?

Or maybe she should just fall to her knees and beg.

This was not a good idea. In fact, this was about as bonehead as one could get without years of planning. Tess turned to run just as the door opened.

"What…?"

Tess froze at the sound of Lacey's voice. She'd answered her own door. Didn't she have underlings to do that for her? Tess turned slowly, trying to smile nonchalantly, as if she wasn't making a colossal ass of herself. "Hi, Lacey."

The woman looked seriously unhappy. As if her face wasn't signal enough, her hand on her highball glass was nearly white with her squeeze. Tess wouldn't be surprised if the crystal shattered. "What are you doing here?"

"Hoping to talk to you."

"Why?"

"May I come in?"

Lacey studied her with a bitter eye. All Tess wanted to do was bolt, but she held steady, using every trick she'd ever learned about acting cool under pressure.

Lacey stepped back, and Tess walked inside.

The brownstone was huge, much bigger than she would have guessed from the outside. In her universe, a place like this would have been split into a bunch of tiny flats. This felt like an airplane hangar.

The white marble floor gleamed under the lights of a chandelier, which would have looked well in the Met. Flowers, the kind Tess saw at five-star hotels, were arranged on three antique tables. God, she'd love to have this account. Well, maybe not.

The most impressive thing, aside from the curving staircase, was the picture on the foyer wall. It looked to Tess like a Picasso. A real Picasso.

"You're in," Lacey said. "What did you want to say?"

Tess forgot about the painting and turned to face the blonde. With her hair pulled back in a loose ponytail, and no makeup, Lacey seemed a bit less intimidating. Didn't seem to help the butterflies in Tess's tummy. "I know you spoke to Jim Cullen about me. That you told him my business wouldn't be a good investment. What I want to know is why."

Lacey's lips curled up slightly. "You're kidding, right?"

"I've never been more serious."

"You think you can just walk in? With no family, no money, no ties? You think membership in this club is that easy?"

"I wasn't aware it was a club."

"It's the most important club there is. It's all about wealth and power. Surely even you can understand the stakes."

Tess took a deep breath, letting Lacey's casual cruelty pass her by like an ill wind. "What I don't understand is how I threaten you. I'm not here to take your place."

Lacey walked over to the flower arrangement in the center of the foyer. She put her glass down on the table, then folded her arms across her chest. Her shirt had a small stain over the right pocket. "Honey, no one can take my place. I'm the keeper of the keys. I know every skeleton in every closet in Manhattan. Why do you think Cullen turned you down?"

"Again, I ask the same thing. How do I threaten you?"

"I would have let you have your moment with Brad. He's really not very important in the scheme of things. But now you want Dash, and that's simply not going to happen."

"Doesn't Dash have something to say about that?"

"He's in lust. It will pass. It always passes."

"So what would be the harm in letting me have my business. If I can't touch you, and I can't have Dash, I must be pretty harmless."

Lacey chuckled. "True. By yourself, you are. But others would see you. Try to be like you."

"You're amazing," Tess said, her fear diminished in the face of such absurd hubris. "And if you think I'm going to let your petty little acts of aggression stop me, you're wrong."

"Am I?"

A surge of anger pulsed through Tess' veins. "Pitifully. I do have Dash, and I will have my shop. I don't need Cullen. Or you. I made it this far on my own, and some pasty little rich snob isn't going to trip me up."

Lacey's eyes widened. "Well, goodness. Aren't you just a Texas terror."

"Damn straight."

Lacey chuckled again. "You go for it, girl. Teach me my place. Show me how you Texans can take on the world. But before you go, I have something I think you should see."

Immediately suspicious, Tess took a step toward the door.

"No, it's nothing fatal. At least, I don't think it is. Are you brave enough, Texas Tess? Can you look at the unvarnished truth and still be so full of righteous anger?"

"Try me."

Laughing out loud, although with no humor whatsoever, Lacey walked toward a pair of ornate French doors. Tess followed reluctantly, not at all sure she hadn't bitten off more than she could chew.

Damn, but the woman needed to be slapped down a few dozen pegs. Arrogant bitch. Who was she to say Tess couldn't have Dash? Jealous, that's all. She wasn't special enough to get someone as wonderful as Dash and…

Tess stopped when she walked into the room. It was a home theater, but unlike any Tess had seen outside *Architectural Digest.* The screen was big enough for a commercial theater, the chairs and couches all Italian leather. The sound of the program filled the space, and Tess noticed a hint of popcorn in the air. The bar on the far side of the room was as grand as everything else. A bottle of citrus vodka held center court.

Lacey picked up a remote control, and clicked Rewind before Tess could make out the program. A few dizzying seconds later, Lacey hit Play, and it took Tess a moment to figure out what she was watching. The Golden Globes. Vaguely, she remembered reading they'd be on, but she wasn't an award show type of gal. The cameras were focused on the red carpet, and she spotted Brad Pitt and Jennifer Aniston basking in the spotlight.

"What is this?" she asked.

"You'll see." Lacey chuckled. "They say it's all about timing. How right they are."

Tess hovered near the door, wanting to get out of this house, back into the fresh, untainted air of Manhattan. Lacey scared her in a way that New York hadn't. This was personalized malice, a bullet with Tess's name on it, and while she talked like a tough Texan, Tess felt like a little kid up against a formidable grownup.

"There," Lacey said.

Tess focused on the screen, seeing him instantly. Dash, smiling, relaxed. Nodding toward the bleacher full of fans, his hand tucked up against the small of Helen Hunt's back. They looked perfect together, equal to Brad and Jennifer in every respect. Tess put her hand on her own stomach, praying she wouldn't get sick.

"You really think you belong with him? That he could possibly want you for anything other than the novelty? You're so far out of your league you can't even buy a map. Go home, Tess. Go back to your little town. Trust me on this, you'll be much happier. This pool has large sharks, hon, and the only thing you've ever fought are guppies. You're not welcome. Is that clear enough?"

Tess swallowed. Then she summoned every ounce of courage she had. "It's clear. But it's also bullshit. This isn't the Old West, and you can't run me out of town."

"You're right. But I can make it damned uncomfortable for you to stay."

"It must be a nightmare being you," Tess said.

"Oh, please. Don't even."

Tess turned to leave.

"Oh, and Tess?"

She stopped, not wanting to.

"You're not even good for a laugh. It's sad, really. You're so much like all his others. Although I have to admit, you fell for his line more quickly than anyone guessed. Usually, he has to work harder before they agree to see him on the sly. Oh, well. He obviously finds you amusing."

Tess almost said the curse she was thinking aloud, but she held off. She was a lady, and no way she was going to let someone like Lacey drag her down. She walked out, keeping her head high and her back straight.

She didn't fall apart until she was at her own front door.

DASH ALMOST TOLD THE limo driver to go to her apartment. He wanted to see Tess more than anything. She'd been on his mind for three days, and the damned thing was, all he could see was a miserable ending for someone he cared too much about. He had to end it. Even though he'd miss her something fierce. Miss her like no other woman he'd ever known.

God, he wanted to be in her bed. In her body. He wanted to feel her nails on his back, hear the way she gasped when he penetrated her, the tremors of her body when she came. He wanted to sleep with her spooned in his arms. To wake up to her smile.

But even he wasn't that selfish. He couldn't be. Not toward her.

How had it happened so quickly? Was it only five weeks ago that she'd simply been the plant lady?

He thought about that night, at the party, in the pool house. She'd been incredible. But he hadn't fallen for her then. That came later. During their long talks at night. Over rocky road ice cream. Sitting cross-legged on her bed, listening to the sounds of sirens pulse through the city.

The limo stopped, and Moe opened his door, but Dash didn't move. He couldn't.

He'd fallen for her.

No way he could kid himself about it. Not now. The truth was out, and it had kicked him in the gut. He was in love with Tess. Only in order to have her, he'd have to give up the only life he'd ever known. Not to mention how many people he'd hurt.

"Sir? Shall I take you to Ms. Norton's?"

He nodded. Even the chauffeur knew the score. Dammit all to hell.

SHE KNEW HE WAS COMING before he knocked. How, she couldn't say, but it was a fact. She'd felt him. Known he was going to come directly from the airport.

And still, she wasn't prepared.

Each knock was like a punch to the stomach. She had to grip the arms of the chair with all her might, hold on so tightly she thought she might tear apart.

If she saw him, she would crumble. The only strength she had was this. One look, one touch, and it would be all over. She'd give in, take him under any circumstances.

He knocked again, louder this time, almost desperately. The tears kept streaking down her face, but she dared not lift a hand to wipe them away.

It wasn't what Lacey had said. She didn't believe the bitch for a moment about Dash. He may have been with a hundred women, but she knew with absolute certainty that her relationship with Dash Black was real, and special, and private and wonderful. She also knew that Dash Black was never meant to be hers.

The pounding on the door grew more insistent.

"Leave," she whispered. "Why can't you just go?"

But when he did, and the silence fell, it was infinitely worse.

"TESS, PLEASE. JUST TALK to me. I don't understand…"

He didn't finish the sentence. He didn't have to. He'd left the same message dozens of times. She wouldn't take his calls, she wouldn't open her door. She even had one of her friends take care of the plants at Noir.

It was driving him crazy.

Yeah, he had planned on breaking things off with Tess, but not this way. Not with this silence. What had happened in the three days he'd been in L.A.? He couldn't help thinking that there was more to it than Tess deciding it wasn't going to work out between them. She wasn't the type to hide from that kind of conversation. At the very least she'd have written him a letter explaining—

He stood up, raked a hand through his hair and headed for the music room. It was late, almost eleven, and he'd taken work home with him from the office, but no way he was going to be able to concentrate.

Maybe he'd find some comfort in his piano. It had worked for him before. He turned on the overhead light, then dimmed it to shadowy softness. He sat on the black bench, stared at the elegant slope of the Steinway. He hardly thought about the ritual of running his fingers over the keys, touching them as gently as he'd touched Tess. At least the piano didn't confuse the hell out of him.

Closing his eyes, he began to play his favorite piece, the one Tess had heard the last time he'd seen her. Pictures of her formed in his mind's eye, and his pain was in the chords and his longing in the vibrations. The music changed. Changed because she wasn't there to hear it.

He had to get to her. There was no other choice. He also had to make some hard decisions about what he'd do once he had her. As he played, one idea kept repeating. One solution that would serve them all, if he could pull it off.

TESS HUMMED AS SHE WASHED her teacup, but it didn't do a damn thing for her spirits. At first, she hadn't recognized the tune. How she'd come to know it so well after hearing it only once was a mystery, but then wasn't everything to do with Dash a mystery? Why had he asked her to the party in the first place? Why had she made love with him? Why couldn't she let him go?

This was inevitable. This pain. She'd known that from the moment she'd agreed to his terms. Eventually, she'd have to move on, live in the real world. The world she'd talked about with Erin and Samantha.

God, whose bright idea was this Man To Do thing? For Erin and Sam, hey, it was no problem. They were normal human beings. Not like her.

Maybe her incredible lack of judgment was a chemical imbalance thing. Wouldn't that be great? Then she could take a pill and find someone safe and nice and regular to marry. Someone named Bill or Tom or Clarence. Someone who watched Helen Hunt on reruns, not across the dinner table.

Dash Black. Please. It wasn't even a real name. Okay, real, but not *real*. Nothing about him was her kind of real. Not the way he kissed her. Certainly not the way he made love.

She realized she'd nearly scrubbed the pattern off her dish. She turned off the water, dried the dish and put it away. Which wouldn't have been a big deal, except now what was she going to do? It wasn't quite midnight, and there was no sleep indicated in the near future. She'd already cleaned out every drawer and closet, and cursed whoever had built this place for the lack of storage space.

She'd tried to read. Uh-uh. TV? Nope. Even old, sad movies couldn't hold her attention for longer than ten minutes. If it had been just a bit earlier, she'd have called Mary, although her friend was so sick of her whining, she'd taken to bringing her knitting when she came over.

Tess flopped on the love seat. She was pathetic. And miserable.

The only decent thing she'd done in the last five days was to find T. Roy Miller. Not only was he a venture capitalist with a sterling reputation and a dynamite track record, he was looking for an investment that fit her business plan like a glove. He'd promised to get back to her in a few days. He'd smiled. Said encouraging things. He'd even flirted a bit. But his biggest plus was that he didn't know Lacey.

Oh, great. Now that conversation dropped on her psyche like two tons of wet cement.

She'd only been over it, say, ten thousand times. If there was ever a murder committed in the foyer or TV room at Lacey's she'd be able to give every detail of the space to the police. Hmm, best not to travel down that road, despite the fact it was the only ray of sunshine in her bleak little world.

Unfortunately, try as she might, Tess couldn't blame this mess on Lacey. Or on Dash. He'd been honest from the start.

She'd walked in with her eyes wide open and her mind completely mired in fantasy. Somewhere, somehow, despite her protests, she had believed things would change. That he would love her. That he'd give up everything for her. Hell, King Edward did it for Wallis Simpson, right? And that was a real, honest to God empire, not a conglomerate of naughty entertainment companies.

The fantasy had been alive and well, growing daily as they'd gotten to know each other. Blossoming with every kiss. It was like emotional kudzu, the vines taking over every bit of sense she'd ever had.

And now, here she sat, her eyes puffy, her hair like something the cat dragged in, her ancient robe tied with someone's old necktie. Pathetic.

Lonely.

So sad, her heart would surely never be glad again. *Oh, Dash. What have you done to me?*

18

DASH FELT LIKE A LOVESICK fool as he walked down the hallway to Tess's apartment. It was Sunday, the night of the big gala, and he had a million things to do, but he didn't give a damn. He hadn't been able to reach Tess for over a week. He should have shaken her off by now. Only, she wouldn't leave.

He stood at the door, listening, but he didn't hear a sound. Until a door shut behind him, making him jump.

"Hey, it's you."

He remembered the oddly dressed girl from the first time he'd been here. "Hi, Mary." Today, she was dressed in farmer overalls, a thick sweater underneath, and heavy black boots that looked like she'd bought them in the Ukraine.

Her head tilted slightly to the left as she eyed him suspiciously. "Did she ask you to come over?"

He could lie, but what would be the point. "No."

"Have you talked to her at all?"

He shook his head.

Mary walked toward him, shoving her hands into the expansive pockets of her getup. "So, tell me, Dash Black. Why are you here?"

His ire rose at the temerity of the question, but at

this stage of the game he had nothing left to lose. "I'm hoping she'll open the door."

"Then what?"

"Shit, I don't know. Maybe if I knew why she'd cut me off without a word…"

"What did you expect?"

He'd done a lot of thinking about that very thing. "More. Unrealistic, I know. Selfish. But I wanted more."

"And what was she going to get out of it. Aside from basking in your glory?"

He winced. "You ought to be a prosecutor. Damn."

"Sorry. Blunt to a fault. But the question remains."

"I want to be with her."

"That's about you."

He leaned against the door, tired, suddenly, to the core. "I'm trying to make it work. I have some ideas, but I'm not sure they'll pan out."

"What do you mean, make it work?"

"I want to be with her, Mary, okay? Not just when work allows me to. And I don't want to see anyone else, even if it is just business."

"Really?"

"Yes, really."

"Wouldn't that entail disrupting your life quite a bit?"

He laughed. "You could say that."

"But you're not sure if you can."

"No. I'm not. There are other people involved. I can only hope."

Mary nodded slowly, still eyeing him in her unsettling fashion. "Okay," she said, more to herself than him. She motioned her head, telling him to step aside. Then she knocked on Tess's door.

The second her knuckles hit wood, his heartbeat accelerated, his chest tightened. A surge of adrenaline made his face hot. He was finally going to see her. Talk to her. Explain—

The door opened. "Oh, shit, Mary, I can't—"

His gaze met hers in a moment outside of time. She looked thinner, paler. Beautiful beyond words. He'd memorized the details of her face, and yet she was somehow new to him. Perhaps because he'd only seen her happy.

"Oh, God," she whispered.

"Talk to him," Mary said. "You're already miserable, so what the hell, right?"

Tess tried to smile, but it didn't work. Christ, the hope in her eyes…

He closed the distance between them but it was only when she touched him, when her hand went to his cheek, that he breathed again. Then she was in his arms, and his lips found hers.

The feel of her was like coming home. He couldn't get close enough, not by a mile. He kissed her, drank her, until she finally pulled back and led him inside. Mary had gone, for which he was grateful, but not nearly as grateful as he felt when the door closed and he was still inside with Tess.

Tess had on worn jeans and a long-sleeved T-shirt. Her hair looked spiky and wild, as if she'd just been in bed. Dash kept staring at her eyes, though. At the redness, the puffiness. She'd been crying very recently.

"I'm sorry," he said.

"For what?"

"For asking you to compromise yourself. I had no business."

"No. You had every right to ask. I thought I knew what I was getting into. But I didn't..."

"What?"

She hugged herself. "I didn't know it would feel like this."

"For what it's worth, neither did I."

She looked down, then slowly lifted her gaze. "I can't, Dash. I can't settle."

"I know. I won't ask you to."

"Then why...?"

"Come here? Because I needed to see you one more time. I couldn't let it go. You have no reason to talk to me, but I needed to try. I've missed you."

She sighed. "This isn't going to change anything."

"I know. But I have one favor to ask you. It's a big one, and I'll understand if you say no. Only, please don't say no."

"What is it?"

He touched her arm, the jolt between them as strong as that first night. "Come with me to the gala."

Her eyes widened. "That's tonight."

"It's in about four hours, actually. Please, Tess, come with me. One last night. One last party."

"I don't know, Dash. I mean, this is hard enough in private."

He needed her to do this. If things were going to go the way he wanted them to, he had to convince her to come. Gripping her arms with his hands, he made his plea. "I need you to be there, Tess. Yes, another incredibly selfish move on my part, but by now you're used to that, right? I need you. I can't put it any plainer than that.''

She looked at him for a long time. The seconds beat along with his heart, and he had to force himself to wait, not push.

Finally, when he knew he couldn't take it another second, she whispered, ''I can't say no to you. That's the problem.''

''Oh, baby, please don't worry. Please. Just for tonight, let's pretend we don't have a prayer, okay? Let's make this the most memorable evening of our lives.''

''I won't have a problem remembering every detail.''

He smiled. For the first time in a long time, he felt hopeful again. If only they could catch a break, this might turn out to be the night that would change them forever.

SHE WORE THE RED dress again.

Her hands shook as she slipped it on, and no amount of deep breathing or positive self-talk could calm her down. This was a mistake of colossal proportions, along the lines of the Edsel or tongue piercing.

The odd thing was, she didn't have any misgivings about attending the gala per se. Something had shifted in her during the last week. Something she hadn't realized until just this second.

Her concern about belonging, about being good enough to be with Dash, was all a bunch of nonsense. Why she'd given it a moment of her time seemed absurd. So what if he dated movie stars. The truth was, she couldn't have him. Period. The end. Whether it was Nicole Kidman or the woman who ran the Laundromat, the end result was that Tess had fallen in love with a man who could never be hers.

She slipped on her shoes, then headed for the bathroom, her pulse racing as she noticed the time. He'd be here in a half hour. Him and his limousine and his chauffer, and it wouldn't have mattered if he'd come on a bicycle because she loved him. Loved him in a way that changed the most important parts of her life.

No longer would she be able to kid about her love life. Her e-mails to Samantha and Erin had already changed. The irony that she'd fallen for the ultimate, card-carrying, number one Man Not To Do Under Any Circumstances wasn't lost on her. Only, now, she didn't want anyone else. Not the most eligible, marriage-minded, daddy-focused, sturdy, dependable handsome guy in the whole U.S.A. could possibly appeal to her now, or in the future.

She'd met him. The *one*. The only.

"Don't cry. Don't you dare cry."

The woman in the mirror ignored the threat, which made it ridiculously hard to put on her makeup. She ended up with lipstick, a little blush, and the ever popular, red-eyed, mascara-smudged look. She didn't give one tiny damn.

When the knock came, she was as ready as she was ever going to get. Which wasn't ready at all.

THE GALA TOOK UP THE entire banquet floor of the Plaza. Dash and Tess had come in the back way, avoiding the gauntlet of cameras in front, but there were still enough photographers inside to fill the pages of tabloids for days to come. Tess had never seen such a gathering of celebrities. It was like going to the Oscars.

Yet all she was terribly conscious of was how Dash held her hand, or touched the small of her back. They could have been anywhere, doing anything. Except for the fact that Dash couldn't take a step without someone stopping him, shaking his hand, wishing him well.

The entered the main banquet hall, and her jaw dropped at the lavish decor. All black and white, with the striking exception of red roses, the room looked otherworldly in its splendor. A rather large orchestra played from a platform at the far side, soothing the masses with a new age melody. Waiters and waitresses darted about handing out glasses of champagne.

The tables had white cloths, black accoutrements and red rose centerpieces. There must have been a hundred tables, at the very least.

Pictures dotted the room, some suspended from the ceiling, some high on the walls chronicled a visual history of Noir, with Dash's father taking center stage. But Dash and Patrick were up there, too. As Dash spoke to Katie Couric, Tess studied his past, his legacy. What on earth had made her think, even for a moment, that she could have him? It was almost laughable.

"Come on," he said, whispering intimately, his warm breath making her shiver. "Let's head over to the stage. I have to find Patrick."

She nodded, and this time they made better time,

because Dash put his arm around her, and spoke to her the whole way across the room. She could barely hear him as he pointed out this celebrity or that picture, but she didn't listen. She simply hugged his waist, felt his body next to hers.

He was by far the most stunning man in a crowd of stunning men. She'd never seen anyone look better in a tuxedo. Women, from starlets to doyennes stared at him with open admiration if not lust.

She thought about that first night. How impressed she'd been with Dash. Things had changed. Not that she wasn't impressed with him, but now it was for completely different reasons. Starting with a bowl of rocky road ice cream.

"I'm going to leave you here for a few moments," he said, nodding toward the head table. "I'll send over a waiter. Be back in a minute." He kissed her on the lips, then he headed toward the back of the room. A woman in an emerald green dress had seen it, and her expression said it all. Surprise. Curiosity.

Tess ignored her and sat down, peering through the crowd for a waiter. Finally, one came by and she took two flutes from his tray. She sipped on the excellent bubbly as she watched the party swirl around her. It was odd, like she was sitting on the outside of a huge glass window, watching, not part of things.

She had no idea how long she'd waited. A half hour? Maybe. But finally, Dash came back. Something had happened. Something good. His demeanor had changed, and his smile was full of excitement.

"Did you miss me?" he asked as he slipped into the seat beside her.

"Desperately."

He chuckled. "I missed you, too." He scooted closer to her, but angled the chair so they almost faced each other. "I need to ask you something."

"What?"

"Why didn't you want to see me?"

Completely caught off guard with the question, she just blinked at him for a moment. "Uh, is this a trick question?"

He shook his head.

She focused on him. On the anticipation in his gaze. "Because I couldn't share you anymore."

He leaned in closer. "Why?"

She took a deep breath. "Because I love you."

His smile broadened. "Man, I was hoping you were going to say that."

"You were?"

He kissed her again, too briefly, then stood up. "Don't go anywhere."

"Okay," she said, but he was already steps away. Her heart raced as her hope soared, but she couldn't put together a coherent thought. What was he up to? What did it mean?

She didn't have to wait long to find out. The music stopped as the microphone on the stage came to life with a burst of feedback. Then Dash's father, looking as elegant as ever, stepped into the spotlight.

She listened to his speech, applauded his achievements, stood up for a standing ovation when he declared his retirement. It all went by in a dizzying haze, as she watched Dash stand next to Patrick just behind their father.

Next came the big announcement. The turning over of the reigns as one man stepped down, and his son took over. Michael's voice trembled as he talked about his son. Only...

Tess had to grab hold of the back of her chair, or she would have fallen down. Because the man who was taking over as the head of Noir Industries wasn't Dash, but Patrick.

The whole room seemed as stunned as Tess, and for a moment, there was this crackling silence. Someone began to clap, and that broke the ice.

Patrick, looking as good as she'd ever seen him, smiling, confidant, stood next to his father. He waited for the applause to die down, and made his own speech about his dad, and about his new role.

Tess kept staring at Dash. He looked in her direction, and finally, they connected across the large space. He smiled, nodded once.

Oh, God.

At the sound of his name, Tess turned her gaze to Patrick.

"My big brother isn't leaving Noir Industries," he said. "He's going to be our CEO, and intimately involved in every decision the company will make. And there are a few other changes in store, as well, but I'll let Dash tell you about those."

Dash walked to the mike amid thunderous applause. He stood next to his family, and she could see the pride on his face and in his stance. He waited until the room stilled, then he found her again as he spoke.

"I know everyone expected me to take over for my dad," he said. "And I would have been proud to do it. I love my father, and I respect him tremendously. He's built an empire out of nothing. He worked tirelessly all his adult life, and I got to bask in his glory for many years. As much as I want to continue his legacy, I believe I can best serve behind the scenes.''

Several members of the crowd announced their displeasure with boos, and Dash held out his hands to quiet them. ''Thanks, I appreciate it. But trust me, Patrick is the right man for the job. He's going to take Noir places we never dreamed about. He is the new face of Noir, and I, for one, couldn't be more pleased.''

The applause was more conservative, but the catcalls had stopped. Tess was still trying to process what she was hearing. Patrick was taking over as spokesman for Noir. It was stunning news, and she could barely let herself think what it meant.

Dash turned to the conductor of the orchestra and nodded. When the music started, Tess closed her eyes to stop her tears. She knew the piece, had heard him play it on his piano. Had hummed the melody over and over again.

When she opened her eyes, she found Dash looking at her. ''In case you're wondering,'' he said, into the mike, ''the reason I decided to step aside isn't because I don't love Noir and all it represents. But because I love you more.''

Tess put her hand to her heart, certain it would beat right out of her chest. He loved her. He *loved her.* So much, he would give up the life he'd always known, the life he'd prepared for from birth. It was too much to believe, too incredible to happen to her.

Tess Norton from Tulip, Texas. Go figure.

''Why don't you come on up, honey,'' Dash said.

It took her a moment to figure out if she could

stand, let alone walk. But she found her feet, and as she made her way to the stage, the crowd parted like the Red Sea. She kept her gaze on Dash, on his smile.

Somehow, she made it to the stairs, didn't trip, and then he was there to hold on to her hand as he led her center stage. He leaned over to the mike. "This is Tess Norton. Soon, I hope, to become my bride."

After a momentary pause, the crowd burst into another ovation, but she hardly heard a thing. Just her heart beating, and his music.

He kissed her then, and nothing else mattered. Nothing. She was with the man she loved. He'd moved heaven and earth so they could be together.

When he finally pulled back, he whispered, "May I take that as a yes?"

She grinned. "You may."

"Phew. That could have been embarrassing."

She laughed as she found herself in Patrick's embrace, and then in her future father-in-law's. Finally, she was back with Dash, who, with a mischievous wink nodded for her to look into the crowd, by one of the open bars. Tess bit her lip to stop from laughing as she caught sight of Lacey, perfectly dressed, exquisitely coifed, looking like she was going to be sick to her stomach. And right next to her was the ever popular Brad, who wasn't looking so well, himself.

Dash squeezed her hand. "How would you feel about going somewhere a little more private?"

"I'd feel wonderful about that."

He wiggled his brows, whispered something to his father, and led her backstage. They didn't stop until they were inside the limo.

That's when he pulled the little velvet box from his

pocket. When he took the dazzling diamond ring and put it on her finger.

"You're the most incredible woman I've ever known," he said. "I want to take the rest of my life to learn everything about you."

"Lucky for you, I'm not otherwise engaged."

He laughed right up until he kissed her.

Epilogue

To: Erin
CC: Samantha
From: TessThePlantLady@hotmail.com
Subject: Saying I Do!

Dearest Friends,
First, a bit of business...I'm financed! No, not by
Dash. I actually managed to get a real live venture
capitalist to put his money and his faith in me. As
soon as the wedding stuff is over, I'm going to start
looking for a shop. Yippee!!

Oh, and speaking of wedding stuff, you'll get the
official invitation in the mail, but this is from my
heart...if it wasn't for the two of you, I never would
have dared. Never would have dreamed. You kept
me going, saved my sanity, helped me believe in
myself. If that isn't friendship, then I don't know what
is.

I love you guys, and I want you to be part of my
wedding. Bridesmaids, anyone? And no, the dresses
won't be horrible, I promise.

I agree that we should open up the group. I know
Mary is going to sign on (I've told you about her)
and I have a couple of other friends who want to
participate.

The MEN TO DO project didn't turn out exactly as I thought, but that's okay. I'm pretty pleased with what did happen. Erin, you and your hubby are doing so well. And Sam? Honey, it's just a matter of time.

Miracles can happen. I promise. Just look at what happened to me.

Love you,
Tess

*   *   *   *   *

*Satisfy your craving for more
Men To Do with the next installment of
this scorching Blaze mini-series!*

Don't miss Isabel Sharpe's
A TASTE OF FANTASY,
available from Blaze in February 2003.

1

From: Samantha Tyler
Sent: Thursday
To: Erin Thatcher; Tess Norton
Subject: Love

What I can't seem to get my brain to stop obsessing over is: How do you know when love is real? I was so sure it was real with Brendan. Zero doubts. Zero cold feet. I stood at the altar and did the Death Do Us Part thing with my heart so full I'm surprised it didn't pop out of my grandma's dress.

If something that good and that right and that perfect, that I believed in it with every ounce of my naïve-assed 20-something passion, could turn out to be nothing more that neurotic unfounded fantasy, how do you know when it's real?

That's why I'm thinking this Men To Do thing might be the way to go right now. I'm not ready for love. Not until I can get my head around this question and get some kind of answer that makes sense.

But I sure as hell could use some sex.
Samantha

◆ HARLEQUIN® *Blaze*™

From: **Erin Thatcher**
To: **Samantha Tyler;**
                Tess Norton
Subject: **Men To Do**

Ladies, I'm talking about a hot fling with
the type of man no girl in her right mind
would settle down with. You know, a man to
do before we say "I do." What do you think?
Couldn't we use an uncomplicated sexfest?
Why let men corner the market on fun when
we girls have the same urges and needs?
I've already picked mine out....

**Don't miss the steamy new Men To Do miniseries
from bestselling Blaze authors!**

THE SWEETEST TABOO by Alison Kent
December 2002

A DASH OF TEMPTATION by Jo Leigh
January 2003

A TASTE OF FANTASY by Isabel Sharpe
February 2003

Available wherever Harlequin books are sold.

◆ HARLEQUIN®
Makes any time special ®

THE BAD GIRLS Club

They're strong, they're sexy, they're not afraid to use the assets Mother Nature gave them....

Venus Messina is...

#916 WICKED & WILLING

by Leslie Kelly

February 2003

Sydney Colburn is...

#920 BRAZEN & BURNING

by Julie Elizabeth Leto

March 2003

Nicole Bennett is...

#924 RED-HOT & RECKLESS

by Tori Carrington

April 2003

The Bad Girls Club...where membership has its privileges!

Available wherever

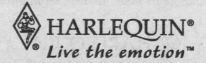

HARLEQUIN®

Temptation.

is sold....

HARLEQUIN®

Live the emotion™

Visit us at www.eHarlequin.com

HTBGIRLS

HARLEQUIN®
Temptation.

South Village Singles

When Suzanne, Nicole and Taylor vow to stay single, they don't count on meeting these sexy bachelors!

ROUGHING IT WITH RYAN
January 2003

TANGLING WITH TY
February 2003

MESSING WITH MAC
March 2003

Don't miss this sexy new miniseries by Jill Shalvis—
one of Temptation's hottest authors!

Available at your favorite retail outlet.

HARLEQUIN®
Makes any time special ®

Visit us at www.eHarlequin.com

HTSVS

There's something for everyone...

Behind the
Red Doors

From favorite authors

Vicki Lewis Thompson

Stephanie Bond

Leslie Kelly

A fun and sexy collection about the romantic encounters
that take place at The Red Doors lingerie shop.

**Behind the Red Doors—
you'll never guess which one leads to love...**

Look for it in January 2003.

HARLEQUIN®
Makes any time special ®

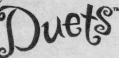
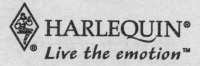